Fabulous Fathers

Go play with your son,

Sami thought. This is probably the last chance you're going to get.

As she watched Clay crouch down and begin to quietly admire Jess's toy, Sami's throat tightened, her eyes filling with unshed tears. *Oh, God, look at them. They're perfect together. Man and boy; father and son.*

In self-defense, she turned away, stood straighter, lifted her chin in denial of the truth that was so evident and took a deep, shuddering breath. Tonight was absolutely the last time she'd permit this kind of folly. Jess and Clay might truly like each other, even fulfill a mutual need, but she couldn't stand to see them together anymore. The rightness of it was far too painful.

Dear Reader,

This month, Silhouette Romance presents an exciting new FABULOUS FATHER from Val Whisenand. Clay Ellis is *A Father Betrayed*—surprised to learn he has a child and has been deceived by the woman he'd always loved.

Long Lost Husband is a dramatic new romance from favorite author Joleen Daniels. Andrea Ballanger thought her ex-husband, Travis Hunter, had been killed in the line of duty. But then she learned Travis was very much alive....

Bachelor at the Wedding continues Sandra Steffen's heartwarming WEDDING WAGER series about three brothers who vow they'll never say "I do." This month, Kyle Harris loses the bet—and his heart—when he catches the wedding garter and falls for would-be bride Clarissa Cohagan.

Rounding out the month, you'll find love and laughter as a determined single mom tries to make herself over completely—much to the dismay of the man who loves her—in Terry Essig's *Hardheaded Woman*. In *The Baby Wish*, Myrna Mackenzie tells the touching story of a woman who longs to be a mother. Too bad her handsome boss has given up on family life—or so he thought.

And visit Sterling, Montana, for a delightful tale from Kara Larkin. There's a new doctor in town, and though he isn't planning on staying, pretty Deborah Pingree hopes he'll make some *Home Ties*.

Until next month, happy reading!

Anne Canadeo
Senior Editor
Silhouette Romance

Please address questions and book requests to:
Silhouette Reader Service
U.S.: 3010 Walden Ave., P.O. Box 1325, Buffalo, NY 14269
Canadian: P.O. Box 609, Fort Erie, Ont. L2A 5X3

A FATHER BETRAYED

Val Whisenand

Silhouette
ROMANCE™
Published by Silhouette Books
America's Publisher of Contemporary Romance

To Joe.
Words are not enough to tell
how much I love you.
They never will be.

 SILHOUETTE BOOKS

ISBN 0-373-19042-5

A FATHER BETRAYED

Copyright © 1994 by Valerie Whisenand

Printed in U.S.A.

VAL WHISENAND

is an incurable romantic, married to her high school sweetheart since she was seventeen. The mother of two grown children, she lives in a house she designed and which she and her husband built together. Her varied interests have led her to explore many fascinating occupations and travel throughout the United States and Canada. Whether her goal is to write another book, learn a foreign language or prevail over tremendous odds to become a winning game-show contestant, her natural tenacity sees to it that she succeeds. Once she makes up her mind, there's no stopping her!

Clay Ellis on Fatherhood...

I thought I had it all figured out—what it would mean to be somebody's daddy. Then I met Jessie.

He made me realize I'd been fooling myself into believing fatherhood would be simple. It isn't. It's awesome!

Holding yourself responsible for the development of a young life is no easy task. It's more like a sacred trust. And it can be scary, especially when you begin to wonder if your ideas of how to raise children have any validity at all.

Truth is, I guess I'm no different from most fathers. I'll muddle through as best I can, love the kid's socks off, try not to be too strict or too permissive— and hope, somehow, he'll turn out okay. I'll consider myself a success, if, when he's grown, I can look at him and say, "There goes a great guy. I'd admire him even if he wasn't my son."

Till then, it looks like it's one day, one surprise, one lesson at a time, for both of us. Before this adventure is over, I'll bet I've learned as much as Jessie has. Well, almost. Maybe fifteen or twenty years from now I'll take him aside and ask him to explain women to me, starting with Samantha Louise Adamson.

Chapter One

"**G**o away!" Peering through the peephole in her front door, Sami saw that her unexpected visitor was standing his ground. Damn. Of all the possible people to appear out of her past, the last one she wanted to talk to was Clay Ellis.

Apprehensive beyond anything she would have predicted, Sami glanced up the stairway toward her son's second-floor bedroom. If Clay continued to pound on the door, he was sure to wake Jess. Already past two years old, the toddler wasn't keen on naps in the first place. And if Jess awoke while Clay was still there...

Running her fingers through her short, ash-blond hair in frustration, Sami jerked open the door. Clay's hand was raised to continue knocking. Her blue eyes widened. Even in faded jeans and a wrinkled chambray shirt with the sleeves rolled up, the all-too-familiar sight of the tall, broad-shouldered man took her breath away.

Darn it. He looked wonderful. Waiting for him to speak, she tugged the hem of her red T-shirt farther down over her white shorts and cursed the fact her casual clothes hugged her curves so well.

One of his dark eyebrows raised, but he didn't smile. "Your telephone number is unlisted or I'd have called first. Something told me you'd come back to this house someday. I catch you at a bad time?"

Her head swimming, Sami spread her feet a little farther apart for balance, stubbornly refusing to let him see how much his arrival had unsettled her. "I was working," she said flatly.

"Ah, yes. The newspaper job. Fortunately, I noticed your byline last week in the *Inland Empire Express*. It did surprise me."

"What is it you want?" The harsh, patently unfriendly tone of her voice shocked her by its intensity.

Eyes she remembered as being such a warm brown, hardened, darkened. "I won't keep you," he said. "You made it clear a long time ago that you wanted nothing more to do with me. Just tell me where my ex-wife is, and I'll leave you alone."

"Vicki?"

He snorted derisively. "Yeah. So far, she's the only ex-wife I have. You remember—short, perky, hair the same blond color as yours, only longer, gorgeous figure and no conscience to speak of."

"Very funny."

Clay had folded his arms across his chest, and Sami mirrored his defensive posture.

"I'm not trying to make you laugh. I need to find Vicki, that's all. As her sister, I figured you'd know where she was."

"I'm not her keeper."

"Not anymore. But you were once and you're all the family she has. Now, where is she?"

"I don't know." It was an outright lie and the falsehood practically stuck in her throat.

Clay's brow furrowed. "The hell you don't."

She reached for the edge of the door, intending to slam it in his face, but he was too quick for her. In an instant his arm shot out. Braced against the heavy mahogany-paneled door, he stared down at her.

"Let go." Acting much braver than she felt, Sami squared her shoulders. In a contest of brute strength, there was no question who would win, yet she had to stand up to Clay and make him go away or her whole happy world could come crashing down around her.

She cast a furtive glance over her shoulder at the empty staircase. Just as in most of the other old, Victorian-style houses she'd visited, the landing faced the entry. If Jess were to wake and come looking for her, she would have a whole lot more questions to answer than simply the whereabouts of her younger sister.

Stepping back, Sami gestured toward the sitting room. "All right. Let's not stand here arguing."

Clay strode past her, leaving in his wake the familiar scent of his after-shave and triggering memories Sami had convinced herself she'd buried beyond retrieval.

She followed. "Sit down."

"I'd rather stand."

"Then at least keep your voice down, okay?"

Glancing past her, he considered her possible reasons for the request. "Why? Is Vicki here? Is that it?"

Sami held up her hands, palms out, in a gesture meant to placate. "No. I swear."

"Then where is she?"

"I already told you. I don't know."

Seeing Samantha Adamson again after so long had done unwelcome damage to Clay's decision to remain resolute. She'd blossomed. Her curves seemed softer, her breasts more enticing, her skin as warmly inviting as ever. And the sweet smell of her hair! He'd been tempted to lean down and place a kiss on her nape as he stormed past her into the house. Those kinds of errant thoughts would never do if he hoped to accomplish his mission.

Abruptly, Clay sat down on the brocade sofa and feigned nonchalance by lacing his fingers behind his head. "So. When did you last hear from your sister?"

"Why?" Unconsciously, Sami had stationed herself between Clay and the stairway leading to Jess.

"Just wondered." He smiled slightly. "I'm not after her to cause her trouble. It's strictly business."

Clay's candid smile, brief though it was, sent Sami's heart into orbit. "What kind of *business* can you have with Vicki? I thought your divorce was final."

"It is." He stretched his long legs out in front of him.

The pose was so familiar it almost brought tears to Sami's eyes. How often had she seen Clay in that very room, relaxing the exact same way? Hundreds? Thousands? Her past came flooding back in a torrent of memories so sweet and poignant she had to look away or chance revealing the depth of her emotions.

Walking to the bay window and looking out at the peaceful, tree-lined street, Sami spoke without turning. "All right. Assuming I believe you, what kind of business can you have with my sister?"

"Still protecting her?" He made a disgusted noise that was more attitude than speech. "Vicki's a big girl now. She doesn't need mothering anymore."

Sami sighed, pivoting slowly to face the man she had loved since they were little more than children. "Vicki is the kind of person who will always need a mama. If I'd been here, you two would never have made the mistake of getting married in the first place." She saw the muscles in Clay's jaw clench.

"If you'd married me instead of dumping me and running off to San Francisco, I wouldn't have been single to start with."

Sami lifted her chin defiantly. "We've been through all that before. I told you, I have no intention of *ever* getting married. I like my single life."

"So you've said." Less comfortable with the recent direction their conversation had taken, Clay's body posture showed the tension he was feeling. Unable to continue pretending ease as well as he'd have liked, he got to his feet and crossed to where Sami stood.

Stopping only a few feet from her, he raised his eyebrows as he studied her face. "The thing you never did was tell me why."

"It's complicated," she countered. "And past history. I don't intend to discuss it with you—now or ever."

He stiffened, fighting a building urge to take her in his arms, remind her just how good they could have been together and show her what she'd given up for the sake of her career. As far as he was concerned, no job was worth the sacrifice of personal happiness. Why Sami couldn't see the truth of that was beyond him.

He stepped back. "You haven't changed a bit, have you?"

"I don't consider that a fault."

"No, I don't suppose you do," he said flatly. "Look. I'll leave my card. Just give Vicki the number and have her call me, will you? I promise you, she'll be glad she did." Reaching into his pocket, he pulled out his wallet and extracted a business card.

"Leave it on the hall table on your way out," Sami said. She didn't think her shaky equilibrium could weather another close encounter with Clay's after-shave. The thought of how his cheek used to feel next to hers sent shivers up her spine.

Starting for the door, he paused, looked back at her as if contemplating a reply, then did as she asked, closing the door quietly behind him.

Suddenly, Sami *had* to sit down. She made the mistake of plopping onto the sofa in the exact spot where Clay had been. His aura was still present. The cushions felt warm to her bare legs; the masculine scent of him lingered in the air.

Pulling a blue throw pillow into her arms, she hugged it tightly. Dear Lord, was she always going to react so strongly to him? Even after more than three long years, the pain of loving him was just as potent as it had been before she'd fled from his pressure toward long-term commitment.

If only he knew, she thought, her shame washing over her and bringing tears to her eyes. Sami gripped the pillow harder. Some secrets were so bad they must never be revealed. Not even for the sake of love.

Sami had tried to go back to her computer terminal after Clay's visit and finish the story she'd been working on for the newspaper, but her powers of concentration were nil. As soon as Jess woke from his nap and toddled into her make-shift office to see what she was doing, she'd shut down the system and quit for the day, deadlines be damned.

Seeing Clay again had focused her thoughts on how important her son was to her in the broadest sense. Even though she'd always considered the child to be a direct gift from God, daily cares too often tended to interfere with their special time together. In reality, Jess *was* her life. He was the only child she would ever have of her very own, and it was vitally important she remember that.

When she'd tucked the tired little boy in for the night, she'd smoothed his dark curls, caressed his cheek and thought longingly of Clay.

* * *

Clay's business card still lay on the hall table where he'd left it when he returned the following afternoon.

Wide-eyed, Sami opened the door in answer to his persistent knocking.

"Well?" he demanded without bothering to say hello.

"Well, what?" She saw his eyes focus past her to the small, mahogany table.

"You didn't give her my card?"

"No. I told you—"

"I know, I know," he grumbled. "You don't have any idea where Vicki is."

"That's right." Sami wasn't about to permit him to come in again. This time Jess hadn't been down for his nap as long, and he might still be awake.

"I don't suppose you'd be willing to phone some of her friends and inquire."

"You could do that as well as I."

"Not without your help. My wife never included me in her circle of personal friends. I guess she thought I was too stuffy for them."

"Or too straight," Sami offered, sorry at once that she'd volunteered the offhanded compliment.

"Yeah." Clay crammed his hands into the pockets of his jeans to keep from reaching out to touch her in spite of himself. *You'd think a man would be smart enough to stay clear of the Adamson sisters after what I've been through,* he mused. He should be. He'd been burned often enough.

"So, will you give me some leads?" he asked with a hopeful half smile.

"I'm sorry. I can't help you," Sami said. The last person she wanted Vicki to talk to was Clay. They had too many dangerous secrets to keep from him. All her irresponsible, scatterbrained sister would have to do was let it slip about Jess and all hell would break loose. Oh, no. Clay wasn't going to get any names or phone numbers out of Sami. Not in a million years.

"Can't? Or *won't?*" His nostrils flared as he began to lose his temper.

"What difference does it make?"

Clay reached for her, his fingers fastening around her wrist and holding tight in spite of her efforts to extricate herself. "What's happened to you?" he asked, a scowl on his face, anger and confusion in his eyes. "We were friends once. How come all of a sudden you're behaving as if I were the one who jilted *you?*"

She struggled against his hold. "I didn't jilt you. I made my decision perfectly clear before I left."

"In a pig's eye."

Wrenching free, she rubbed her wrist with her opposite hand to keep from letting Clay see how badly she was shaking. "You were just too stubborn to listen to me. Like now. Read my lips. I don't know where Vicki is and if I did, I wouldn't tell you."

"Why the hell not?" Clay shouted. "What have I ever done to you—or to your crazy sister, for that matter? All I tried to do was be your friend."

The guilt that stabbed at Sami was enough to make her soften her reply. "It seems to me you had a whole lot closer relationship in mind than that."

"So? What's wrong with love? There was a time when you seemed to appreciate what I was offering you."

"Never." She shook her head, her soft curls bobbing. "Besides, it sure didn't take you long to find a replacement once I was gone."

Clay took a deep breath and released it with a noisy whoosh. "Ah. Your sister again. Look, I admit I made a mistake in marrying her."

"I could have told you that. As a matter of fact, I did tell Vicki. If you'll recall, that was when she stopped speaking to me."

"Yeah, I remember. I just thought maybe, since we were divorced, she'd have forgiven you."

Chewing on her lower lip, Sami thought about the tearful scene that had reunited her with a desperate Vicki. Thank God she had come to Sami for help instead of doing what she'd threatened. Sami's throat tightened, her mouth suddenly dry, her hands trembling noticeably.

Clay extended his right hand in a peacemaking gesture. "Look, Sami, I'm sorry if I upset you. I just didn't know where else to turn. I suppose my next move should be to hire a private detective."

When she didn't reach out to accept his hand, he lowered it and shrugged. "Okay. I get the picture. If I do locate your sister, do you have any messages for her?"

Sami could only shake her head. Clay must *not* find Vicki. Jess's future depended on it. She forced herself to face the truth. Much more was at stake here than a simple missing person. If she didn't want to end up a lonely old woman with no one in the world to care about her, she'd better make darned sure Clay Ellis didn't hire a private investigator and locate his flighty ex-wife.

"Don't bother with a detective," she said. "I'll see what I can do."

The following morning Sami arranged for Jess to spend the entire day safely sequestered next door as part of Eleanor Truesdale's large brood. Clay Ellis had always been a methodical person, so predictable it was scary. Chances were very good that since he'd called on her every afternoon for two days straight, he'd continue to repeat the pattern. So far, she'd been extraordinarily lucky to have kept Jess's existence a secret from him. If Clay dropped in again as she supposed he would, the safest thing to do was make sure the boy wasn't even home.

Growing more uneasy as the hours passed, Sami had begun to wonder if her precautions had been for nothing, when she heard a forceful, now familiar, knock. Of course Clay had returned. Why not? Like an idiot, she'd virtually promised to help him. The trouble was, she had no idea what to do next and she knew she couldn't keep stalling forever. Sooner or later, the man was going to get tired of waiting.

Sami opened the door without checking through the peephole and her jaw dropped.

"Hi," he said, smiling and extending the bouquet of green-tissue-wrapped flowers he'd brought. "Daisies. I remembered."

"So you did." She accepted the gift. "Thanks."

"You're welcome." Glancing past her, he eyed the house's cool interior. "Redlands sure gets hot in the summer, doesn't it? May I?"

"Umm, sure." Making her way down the hall past the stairway, she headed for the kitchen. "I'll just go put these in water."

"I'll help you."

"That's not necessary. Really, I . . ."

Sami didn't have to look behind her to know Clay was following. She could sense his presence the way she always had. It was as if she possessed a private radar tuned exclusively to the vibrations emanating from Clay Ellis. Even in high school, when Clay was a senior and she a lowly freshman, she'd been tuned in to him. To his credit, he hadn't seemed to mind. Then, when her parents had been killed and she'd been shuttled from foster home to foster home . . .

Sami shivered.

"Hey. It's cool in here, but not *that* cold." He leaned around her to look at her face. "Are you all right?"

"I'm fine."

"Good. Then we can get started calling Vicki's friends."

Ignoring his comment, she took a fluted white glass vase from a high cupboard, filled it with cold water and arranged the daisies. Vase in hand, she turned and headed back toward the front of the house.

Once again, Clay followed. Sami was wearing a dress today, he noted, one of those brightly colored summer things with narrow straps and a full skirt that stopped at her knees. She looked as enticing as ever, a fact his body hadn't failed to note, as well.

Forcing himself to concentrate on the financial mess he would be stuck in if he didn't locate Vicki, he managed to calm his treacherous libido. Samantha Adamson had always had a special place in his heart, he reminded himself, even if he hadn't had the pleasure of making love to her.

In the back of his mind he flirted with the idea that the future might provide opportunity to correct their prior lack of physical intimacy. At the same time, he remembered how adamant she'd been about never getting married and how he'd grieved her loss when she'd chosen a job in San Francisco over staying near him.

Then there was the problem of Vicki. Though Sami might have been persuaded to change her mind about spending her life with him under other circumstances, the fact that he'd once been her brother-in-law had probably ended his chances for good.

He watched her place the vase on the buffet in the dining room, sidestep around the oval table and proceed into the sitting room where she perched nervously on the edge of a Queen Anne chair, smoothed her skirt and clasped her hands in her lap.

Clay chose the comfort of the sofa. "So. Where shall we begin?"

"Begin what?"

Leaning forward, his elbows on his knees, he stared at her, trying to read her expression. "Was I dreaming yesterday or did you say you'd help me?"

"I said I'd see what I could do."

"Well?"

"Well, what?"

He shook his head. "I feel like I'm caught in one of those TV comedy routines where there's always one poor guy who has no idea what the hell is going on."

"Nothing's going on," Sami insisted. "I've been thinking about your problem, but nothing helpful came to me." *That much is true.* Her conscience was shrieking epithets in her mind, demanding she at least admit to Clay she had no real intention of putting him in touch with her sister.

Getting to his feet, he walked across the room and back, using the time and exertion to get better control of his temper. He wasn't about to reveal details of the financial quagmire he was floundering in—especially not to Sami. She'd always seemed proud of his accomplishments, in the military, in college and later in business. The truth was, she'd given him the incentive to strike out on his own sooner than he might have otherwise. Aiming to prove himself, he had done so, only to find he no longer had someone special waiting to share his success.

Clay faced her, his arms folded across his chest. "What am I going to do with you?"

She quirked a smile. "Hopefully nothing."

"You *do* know where Vicki is. I can see it in your eyes."

"Nonsense." Sami lowered her gaze and stared at her hands.

"Is it? You never could lie worth a damn. At least, not to me."

"Clay, I . . ." *I what?* she asked herself. *I lie just fine? I can't let you find my sister? I still love you something fierce?*

I have a son? She blushed, color warming her cheeks. "Never mind."

"You'll be doing me a great favor if you help me," he urged. "Let Vicki phone me. She can set up a meeting anywhere she wants and I'll be there. Only, don't wait long or it'll be too late."

"I can't..."

"Yeah, yeah. I know. You can't get in touch with Vicki. You said that before."

Sami rose to walk him to the door. "I'm really sorry. I just don't think I can help you right now. If you'll be patient, maybe I'll come up with something—you know, one of my bright ideas."

Pausing to stare down at her, he fought the urge to skim the backs of his fingers over her nearly bare shoulders. "I guess I never have understood you, have I, Sami? For a long time I thought we were the ones who'd wind up together, but you never felt the same way, did you?"

"Things worked out for the best," she said.

"Did they?" Clay halted just inside the now open front door, followed his more basic instincts and grasped her shoulders to keep her from retreating.

Sami scrutinized him, watching as he tilted his head slightly, the way he always used to when he was preparing to kiss her. *Turn your face away!* she told herself. *Don't let this happen.* But her body refused to obey.

The touch of Clay's lips was light, brief and so moving, Sami found herself swaying in his grasp.

"Tell me you hated that," he said huskily.

The electricity sparking between them was intense, palpable. Denying it would be foolish. "I never said there wasn't a physical attraction between us," she countered. "But that's not enough."

"It's a start."

"Not for us, it isn't."

Nodding, yet visibly saddened, Clay released her and turned to go.

The sight of Eleanor Truesdale scurrying across the lawn and climbing the front steps right in Clay's path took Sami's breath away. Worse yet, the woman was balancing a teary-eyed Jess on one hip and dragging her own son, Travis, along by his hand.

It was obvious from all the whimpering and grimacing going on that Travis was in pain. Clay stepped aside for the matronly blond, and Sami hoped against hope he'd go ahead and leave once his way was clear.

Eleanor thrust Jess at Sami. The little dark-haired boy wrapped his arms around Sami's neck and clung tightly, hiding his face in the hollow of her shoulder.

"It wasn't Jess's fault," Eleanor said rapidly. "They were playing in the backyard and somehow Travis got a knot on his head the size of one of my Bennie's golf balls. Anyway, his pediatrician wants to see him just to be sure it's not serious. Tricia and Tiffany are at a friend's house and Tommy's playing soccer, so you don't have to worry about them, but I can't take Jess with me. I know I promised..."

"It's okay," Sami said quickly, hugging the upset toddler to her. "I can watch him. Mr. Ellis was just leaving."

Eleanor seemed oblivious to Sami's response. The nervous energy Travis's injury had triggered bubbled over as she smoothed the four-year-old's hair back from his forehead. "What a knot! Boy, I tell you, if Jess doesn't turn your hair gray by—"

"You'd better get that little guy to the doctor," Sami interrupted before Eleanor could be more specific. So far, there was still a good chance Clay would assume she was merely baby-sitting for a neighbor in an emergency. Sami started to walk her friend across their common lawn to her car. "Call me if you need anything else and let me know how brave Travis is." She smiled down at the tow-headed child. "I'll bet he doesn't even cry anymore."

Travis, tears staining his cheeks, looked up at Sami with resolve. "I won't. I'm not a baby."

"I know you're not," Sami told him. "Stop by when you and your mama get home and I'll see if I can scare you up a homemade chocolate-chip cookie."

Eleanor lifted her son into place in the car, fastened his seat belt, then circled the old blue Chevy to get in behind the wheel. "Save a cookie for me, too. Once this is over, I'll need a cup of coffee and some of your soothing goodies."

"It's a deal. Got your purse?" Sami asked. Eleanor may have been a mother much longer, but when one of her brood was hurt or in trouble, all her common sense vanished.

"In the back seat," she said. "Thanks."

Sami raised her hand to wave, and Jess did the same. As the car drove away, Sami glanced back at her own home.

Clay Ellis stood in the shade of her porch, and it didn't look like he intended to leave till she returned. Urging Jess to lay his head against her shoulder, she stroked his dark curls and walked slowly back toward Clay, all the while trying to remember Eleanor's exact words to see if they'd given anything away. Whatever further conversation she and Clay had, it must not refer to Jess if she could help it.

Sami paused at the base of the steps, squinting into the bright sunlight and shading her eyes with her free hand as she spoke. "You can see I'm going to be a bit busy this afternoon."

Frowning, he came down the stairs. "Okay. I can take a hint. I'm leaving."

Sami squeezed her son in a tight, protective hug as Clay stormed past. Her heart was threatening to break at the pain on her old friend's face, the anguish in his eyes. The only thing holding her together was the small boy in her arms.

When Clay paused and looked at her, Sami held her breath and faced him stoically. She hated lies with a passion, yet what choice did she have? Jess was the innocent party in a series of adult mistakes. With her as guardian of his future, he would at least have an ally who was totally dedicated to his happiness.

Thinking back, Sami shuddered in spite of the hot sun beating down on her bared shoulders. If she hadn't intervened, Vicki, wanting her impending divorce to be a quick, clean break with Clay, would have gone ahead with her planned abortion, and the loving child Sami held to her breast wouldn't even exist. The vivid thought made her sick to her stomach.

Clay had reached his black BMW and was opening the door. Sami sighed in relief. Placing a kiss on the top of Jess's head, she whispered, "What a good boy you are. Shall we go have a snack?"

Jess's little head snapped up, a grin spreading across his face. "Cookies?"

Laughing softly, Sami nodded. "Cookies."

"Oh, boy," he shouted, his shrill voice carrying in the still, summer air.

Sami shushed him with a finger to his lips. "Quiet down, honey."

"Why?" The child's attention turned to the tall man who had paused by the side of his open car door. "Who that?"

"That's Mr. Ellis," Sami said.

Shyly, Jess waved. To Sami's surprise, Clay raised a hand in reply. Watching him slowly settle himself into the driver's seat, she felt enough relief to turn and climb the porch steps.

"Love you," Jess said, wrapping his pudgy arms tightly around her neck.

The moisture in Sami's eyes was a mixture of happiness and sorrow. "I love you, too, honey." She purposely didn't look back as she set the child down at their front door.

"Cookies, Mama! Cookies!" he shouted.

So loud. So clear. So *damning*. Sami whirled, hoping Clay hadn't overheard. One look at his face told her that her wishes were for naught.

The BMW was still parked in her driveway, its motor off, windows rolled down. Behind the wheel, Clay sat motionless, staring at her, the shock, condemnation and disappointment in his eyes so impassioned it made her cringe all the way to her soul.

She heard him curse softly as he turned the key to start the car. Jamming it into reverse, he backed out into the street, shifted gears and sped off, tires squealing.

Overcoming her momentary surprise at his turbulent reaction, Sami was running in frantic pursuit of the car before she had time to stop herself. One hand raised, reaching out to him, she raced across the lawn, down the driveway and out into the street.

"Clay! Wait, I—"

Her arms fell to her side, her shoulders slumping. Clay's car was turning the corner. He hadn't seen her wave, hadn't heard her cries.

Breathing raggedly, Sami realized just how lucky she'd been that Clay had gotten so far away before she'd lost control. For a few dangerous moments she'd reacted with a surge of pure emotion and forgotten everything except how deeply she cared about him.

Her heart pounding with clear understanding of what she'd almost done, Sami turned back toward the old Victorian two-story and the life she'd chosen. She had duties. Responsibilities. There was a wonderful little boy waiting for her to make cookies.

Chapter Two

Clay drove around the Redlands, Riverside and San Bernardino areas for hours after leaving Sami's house. When he finally parked his car and went into a coffee shop, he found he couldn't recall anything at all about the territory he'd covered.

He slid into a red-cushioned booth in a far corner of the nonsmoking section, ordered apple pie and coffee, then stared blankly at the fluted paper place mat and the food the waitress placed in front of him. In his unsettled mind, all he could focus on was the child's happy shouts.

Mama. The little boy had called Sami, *Mama.*

Clay's gut wrenched, his nostrils flaring, as he lectured himself about accepting reality. This was the nineties. Women didn't feel they had to get married in order to bear children anymore. He knew that. So why was it tearing him up to know that Samantha Adamson was one of those modern women?

Because he'd once offered her marriage and a family and she'd turned him down flat, he concluded. As a younger man, he'd imagined that he and Sami would one day become husband and wife. Instead, she'd run from commitment as if he were proposing lifelong servitude.

Worse yet, she'd refused to let *him* make love to her, then gone out and gotten herself pregnant! That was what galled him the most, he supposed. Another man had enjoyed the lovely body she'd denied him.

Clay remembered vividly how Sami had behaved whenever they drew close to intimacy. The last time had been the worst, by far. They'd spent a quiet evening in the same house on Cheney Street where she was again living. Vicki was out on a date so he and Sami had the place to themselves.

"Can I get you another cup of coffee?" she'd asked, clearly jittery.

"No, thanks." She was wearing a soft pink blouse and a flowing skirt that he'd thought made her look like an angel. Attributing her nervousness to their opportunity to become lovers that very night, he'd fought hard to keep any display of his own excitement to a minimum.

Patting the cushion next to him, he'd suggested, "Come sit here by me."

Sami had complied, her spine stiff, her posture anything but relaxed as he put his arm around her.

"Don't be scared, honey. I won't hurt you."

"It's not that."

"Then what's wrong?"

"Everything." There was a noticeable catch in her voice.

Clay pulled her closer to nestle against his shoulder and gently caressed her arm through the soft pink fabric. "There's nothing you and I can't handle together, Sami. You know that. We're a great team. Always have been."

"I want us to stay friends."

He'd laughed at her then, instead of taking what she said seriously, never dreaming she was preparing to leave town. To leave him. "We'll always be friends, honey. You'll see. After the kids come along, we'll still make time to be alone together, just like now."

Instead of agreeing, Sami had begun to weep bitterly, and he'd held her, murmuring soothing words till she finally quieted. All along he'd assumed she feared marriage because of her unhappy childhood and the overwhelming burden of raising her younger sister alone for so many years. Now, he didn't know what to think. She'd continually put off *his* sexual advances with the excuse she wanted to remain a virgin.

He snorted derisively. *Look at her now. Some virgin.* Throwing the money for his untouched food down on the table, he stalked out of the restaurant and back to his car.

The thing that made him the maddest was that he'd been such a gentleman with Sami. Gentleman? Try chump, jerk, fool. While he was busy being Mr. Nice Guy, some other bastard had jumped her bones and gotten her pregnant. The image of that happening knotted Clay's guts.

He shifted the car into gear and roared out of the parking lot. What he *ought* to do was go back to the Adamson house and tell Samantha just what he thought of her and her pseudomorals.

What good would that do? he asked himself, trying to deal sanely with what he'd recently learned without being judgmental.

Instant acceptance of Sami as a single mother not only wasn't easy, he found it wasn't possible. At least, not yet. Maybe in a few days, when he'd cooled off, he'd stop by and see her again. Meet the kid. Force himself to behave in a civilized manner.

To his surprised he found his vision clouding. Pulling to a stop at the side of the road, he cursed and beat his fists against the steering wheel. Mentally, he thought he'd released Sami and ended his love for her years ago. Now he could see he'd done nothing of the kind. In his heart, Samantha Adamson was his woman—always had been—always would be.

And if he ever found out who had hurt her and left her, alone and pregnant, he'd gladly beat the SOB to a pulp.

Eleanor's boy, Travis, had a mild headache and a bruise on his forehead, but fortunately no concussion. He'd collected his chocolate-chip reward for bravery and gone upstairs to play with Jess while Sami and his mother talked in the kitchen over coffee.

"I don't know why you're not petrified of those stairs," Eleanor said. "My kids would have broken their necks if I'd let them go up and down at that age like Jess does."

"Being raised in this house helped," Sami told her. "Vicki and I both learned how to negotiate the stairs without falling. Teaching Jess the right way to do it was easier than having to watch him every minute or put gates at the top and bottom."

"I suppose so. You're lucky he's athletic and such a quick learner. My kids are all klutzes."

Sami smiled. "Maybe Jess is just a bit more cautious."

"Takes after his mother," Eleanor observed.

Sami's throat tightened. Would she always be so fearful of discovery? she wondered. Lately, it seemed as if every other sentence reminded her she wasn't Jess's natural mother. The truth was, the little boy did take more after her than he did Vicki, which was a miracle in itself.

"Thanks—I think," Sami finally said. Picking up the plate of cookies, she offered more to Eleanor.

"Just one," the plump woman said, taking two instead. "Tell me. What was Jess's father like?"

Sami nearly dropped the plate. "What?"

"Jess's father. You never talk about him, and I was curious." She paused, blushing. "Of course, if you don't know..."

The suggestion that she'd been so loose with her favors that she didn't know who had supposedly fathered her child caused Sami acute embarrassment. Rather than relate even a minor portion of the real story to her nosy neighbor, she merely said, "He was quite an athlete in college. I guess Jess takes after him."

"I guess so. Do you ever see him?"

"No." Another lie. Another intense pang of guilt.

"You should let him visit. He may be a stinker, for all I know, but he still has a right to get to know his son."

He doesn't know he has a son, Sami thought, her mind in such a turmoil she wasn't sure for a moment if she'd actually spoken the words or not. The placid look on Eleanor's face told her she'd kept silent, thank goodness.

"Sometimes we have to do what's best for the child," Sami said, "no matter who else may be hurt."

"I suppose." Eleanor carried her cup to the sink and rinsed it out. "Well, I'd better be taking my holy terror and leaving you in peace. Tommy and the girls will be home soon, and I have to start dinner. Thanks for the treat."

"You're welcome. Thanks for watching Jess for me this morning."

"No problem. Once I got a peek at that guy you were with, I could understand why you'd want privacy. What a hunk!" Leaning closer, she cupped her hand around one side of her mouth. "Don't tell my Bennie I said so, but I'll trade, if you're interested."

"Clay's not mine to trade," Sami said, joining her friend in a chuckle. "He was my sister's husband."

"Was? Or is?"

"Was. They're divorced."

"So go for it. At least he's already broken in."

"Husbands are not like shoes," Sami countered. "I'd rather have a new one than a used one. That is, if I planned to marry at all."

The shorter woman nodded. "Maybe you've got the right idea after all. Men can be a real pain sometimes."

A pain in the heart, Sami admitted ruefully. *A real pain in the heart. Like Clay.* She took a deep breath. No. Not simply *like* Clay. The pain she was feeling was directly because of him. Seeing Clay again had reminded her how much she'd given up in order to keep the two secrets that had shaped her life until now.

If she'd ever been able to bring herself to permit any man to make love to her it would have been Clay, without a doubt. Yet if he'd been given free access to her body he'd have learned the terrible fact that she wasn't unsullied like he'd thought, and the result would have been the same...she would have lost him forever.

Then there was Jess, the biggest, most important secret of all. Vicki hadn't been sure who his father was, but the moment Sami had lain eyes on the newborn, she'd known. He had Clay's eyes, Clay's hair...Clay's loving nature.

Lacking the maternal instinct that Sami possessed to an extreme, Vicki had gladly turned her son over to her sister to raise. It was fair in a twisted sort of way. The woman who loved Jess's daddy with all her heart had become his only child's nurturer and protector.

But was she being fair to Clay? Sami asked herself. He was the one who had once talked incessantly about having a family, while here he was, divorced and in his thirties, with none of his hopeful dreams fulfilled.

Still, it wasn't really her problem, Sami argued. She hadn't forced Clay to marry Vicki, nor had she caused their divorce. The fact that Vicki found herself pregnant after she and Clay had officially separated wasn't Sami's fault, either. All she'd done was convince her sister to bear the child instead of disposing of it. Surely saving a tiny life couldn't be wrong, could it?

Rationalizing, she supposed she would have to think up a convincing fairy tale to tell Clay when he showed up again—if he did. The look on his face when he'd heard Jess call her Mama was so tortured it was possible he'd avoid her from now on.

Unless he really did need to reach Vicki, Sami added, considering for the first time that Clay might have been lying about his reasons for continually dropping by. Suppose he'd merely hoped to rekindle an old flame? What then?

She tensed. None of her original reasons for holding him at arm's length had changed. Physical traumas of her youth had left her scarred in more ways than one, the most concrete being her inability to bear children. She could never wish that punishment on a man like Clay, who yearned so for a family.

Neither could she chance his finding out who Jess's birth mother was. If he did, sooner or later it would occur to him that it was possible he'd been the one to impregnate Vicki, and then there was no telling what he'd do.

Sami shuddered. The tale she told Clay about Jess's conception and birth would have to paint her in such a bad light he'd never want to see her again. It was the only answer. The only way she could be sure he'd go away and never come back.

Clay was en route home, over the Cajon Pass to Victorville, when he suddenly had an undeniable urge to go back and confront Sami. All the way up the highway he argued with himself that he had no business chastising her, no right to feel cheated, yet he did. In spades. Perhaps if he returned immediately to Redlands, as his heart urged, the act of taking control of the situation would allow his restless mind to unwind.

Using the first available off ramp, he started back down into the valley, oblivious to the heavy traffic, the late hour or the fact he hadn't eaten since breakfast.

His deep-seated need to know more about the boy drove him relentlessly. It was after 9:00 p.m. when he finally turned onto Cheney Street and pulled up in front of the Adamson house. There was one light on in the kitchen and another upstairs. Good. Sami was still up. At least he wouldn't have to wake her.

He slammed the car door and scaled the steps to the porch almost at a run. Sami jerked open the door before he had a chance to knock. Although she'd traded the becoming sundress for blue jeans and a loose T-shirt, she still looked damnably attractive. Raising one eyebrow, he regarded her with curiosity.

"I heard your car," she explained, blocking the doorway with her body. "What do you want?"

"An explanation."

"For what?"

"You know damn well what."

She hardened her heart in self-defense. "I don't owe you any such thing."

"I say you do. Who was he?" Clay demanded.

"He who?"

Clay gritted his teeth. He hadn't driven all the way back to Sami's to play guessing games. "All right, I'll spell it out for you. Who is the boy's father?"

"That's none of your business." Sami had begun to tremble and had to grasp the edges of the doorjamb to steady herself. The fanciful story of Jess's origins she'd been creating in her imagination fled in the face of reality.

"Isn't it? You wouldn't let me touch you. Said you wanted to *save* yourself. Swore you liked your single life. And now here you are with a son. Was I that unappealing, Samantha? Were you just sparing my feelings?"

"No!" Oh, Lord, he looked so hurt, so disappointed. What could she possibly do to assuage his pain? Her own intensified when she realized there was nothing she could do—dared do—to help Clay understand.

"Oh, really?" Fists clenched, he asked, "Are you going to let me in or are you coming out?"

"What for? We have nothing more to discuss."

"I think we do, Ms. Adamson." Taking her arm, he pulled her out onto the porch. "You're going to tell me what happened to make you change your mind about having sex, for one thing."

"Keep your voice down." She wrenched away.

"All right." In a harsh whisper, he continued. "So, who did you finally sleep with, Sami? And why the hell didn't you use protection?"

"That's none of your business," she countered, glaring at him.

"Did you love him?" he asked after a long pause, his voice husky, throaty with emotion.

That was the easiest question he'd posed in a long time. "Yes," she said. "I loved Jess's father."

The answer hit Clay between the eyes like an actual blow. Well, he'd asked for it, hadn't he? Like a fool he'd expected her to deny having deep feelings for another man, and like an even bigger idiot, he'd been surprised when she'd admitted the opposite was true.

He sobered. *Okay.* If that was how it was, then that was how it was. At least she'd given herself to someone else for love. That was a better motive than plain old animal attraction. Or was it?

Clay replayed Sami's last words in his head and picked out the name he'd heard her use. "Jess?" he asked. "Is that what you call the boy?"

Sami nodded.

"How old is he?"

"Two and a half." She didn't see how that smidgen of information could hurt, especially since an educated guess would have provided essentially the same answer.

Seeming more resigned, Clay nodded. "He's a beautiful child."

"Thank you."

A shadow passed over his face before he added, "Oh, Sami, why couldn't he have been ours?"

Sensing the rapid shift in Clay's mood, from anger to anguish, she realized he was far more dangerous to her precarious emotional state when he was acting tender and remorseful than when he was shouting at her. She must not allow herself to weaken.

"You assume too much," she told him flatly, struggling to keep her tone strong, forceful. "You always did. I explained over and over again that I never intended to get married and you kept talking as if we were going to anyway." Her voice broke. "Damn it, Clay, you have no right to act like you own me."

"Don't I?" Taking two quick steps closer, he pulled her into his arms, one hand grasping her jaw and raising her face to his. "I was too easy on you before, wasn't I? Too soft. Too polite. Too nice. If you didn't want a gentleman for a lover, you should have said so."

Before she could reply, he lowered his mouth to hers in a punishing, demanding kiss that stole her breath away.

Suddenly, unreasonable fear shot through her and she stared up at him. For one horrible instant she had flashed back to when she was sixteen and one of her foster fathers had forced himself on her while she slept. Awakening abruptly, she'd tried to scream for help, but he'd clamped his hand over her mouth and threatened to harm eight-year-old Vicki if Sami didn't surrender. What could she do? With their parents both dead, Vicki had no one left to protect her but her big sister. Sami had shut her eyes, held her breath and tried to block out what was happening.

Years later, the lingering shame of that awful night remained. So did the scars. All it took was one tiny incident to trigger the tremendous sensation of guilt she'd tried so hard to rid herself of. When Clay grabbed her and kissed her so forcefully, her memory had automatically revived the clear, ugly details of her abuse. The most amazing thing was, she wouldn't have expected that kind of behavior from him.

In all the years she'd known Clay Ellis, Sami had never experienced any form of cruelty at his hands. Far from it. He'd been more like a big brother to begin with, and as they grew older, she'd come to love him unequivocally, even though she knew nothing concrete could ever come of it.

And now? Had she driven him to this—this bestiality? Was she the reason he'd changed so drastically? Looking up into his eyes, she had her answer. God help her. It was true. It had to be. It didn't matter that she'd meant him no harm. On the contrary, she'd left Southern California so he would feel free to make a good life for himself without her. And *now* look at him! If he'd turned into a monster, it was her fault as much as his.

Cascades of bitter tears began to course down Sami's cheeks as soul-wrenching sobs racked her body. Gulping air, she twisted her head away, intending to somehow find the strength to force him to release her.

Such strenuous efforts weren't necessary. Clay had already let go and stepped back. "Sami, I—"

"Leave...me...alone," she ordered, gasping for breath and covering her flaming cheeks with her hands.

He reached out to her. "Wait—"

Barely able to see through her tears, Sami stumbled toward the sanctuary of her house, slammed the heavy mahogany door behind her and locked it.

Giving in to the soul-wrenching agony she felt, she permitted overwhelming sorrow and guilt to encompass her as she sank to the floor, weeping inconsolably.

Clay just stood there on the other side of the door, listening to her cry and hating himself for making it happen. Of all the possible reactions to his advances, he certainly hadn't expected another episode of hysterics. Not after all she'd obviously been through in the past few years. Sami had to really loathe him to have become so upset over one stolen kiss.

Not that it was right to take what she didn't freely give, he reflected. The trouble was, he'd totally misread her. If she'd been half as excited by his presence as he was by hers, there wouldn't have been a problem. Therefore, it was clear-cut she wasn't sexually or emotionally attracted to him—probably never had been.

As the correctness of his deductions settled in, Clay felt an ache in his heart that penetrated all the way to his spirit. Sami had tried to tell him she didn't love him over and over, and he'd refused to listen. Well, he'd heard her now. Unless she expressed a definite change in attitude, he'd have to leave her strictly alone in the future.

He cursed. Now that he'd been near her again, touched her, held her in his arms, ignoring his feelings was going to be harder than ever.

Hard? he repeated to himself. Hell, it was going to be damn near impossible.

Chapter Three

Clay purposely let three days of cooling-off time elapse before he tried to see Sami again. Even then, it took some pretty complicated mental calisthenics to bring him back for another round of verbal sparring. Although he recognized the machinations of his mind for what they were, he accepted the validity of his basic conclusions. Sami didn't care for him.

He did, however, have a solid excuse for returning to the Adamson house. In all the furor about Jess, Clay had completely overlooked his original motive for coming to Redlands. He still desperately needed to find his ex-wife . . . or else.

One more week, he promised himself, slowly climbing the stairs onto the wooden porch. One more week and he'd break down and hire a detective to locate Vicki. In the meantime, there was no reason why he shouldn't keep bugging Sami about it, was there? Besides, he owed her a king-size apology. The missing Vicki gave him a perfectly logical reason to drop by and make his peace.

This time, his knock on Sami's front door was more temperate. Nevertheless, it echoed through the lower floors of the old house as if he'd pounded.

Not caring that it was the middle of summer rather than spring, Sami had sent Jess outside to play in the enclosed backyard and embarked on a wildly frenetic housecleaning spree, desperately seeking something constructively physical to do after her upsetting confrontations with Clay.

As a result, she answered the door in a paint-splattered, oversize shirt, cutoff jeans and run-down tennis shoes. He, on the other hand, was dressed neatly in dark slacks and a blue short-sleeve shirt. Looking him up and down and denying she was actually glad to see him, she made a sour face.

The consternation evident in her expression made Clay grimace. "Hi."

Hands on her hips, Sami scowled at him. "This is ridiculous. It's getting so I'm afraid to come to the door. I ordered a pizza last night and about jumped out of my skin when the poor delivery boy knocked. He probably thinks I'm some kind of a nutcase."

"Probably." Clay managed a half smile. Darned if she didn't look about twelve years old in that silly getup. "You have a smudge of dirt on the end of your nose," he said, extending a forefinger in her direction.

"Is that what you're here for—to inspect my nose?" she asked, stepping out of reach and rubbing at the supposed smudge with the back of her hand.

"No. I basically came to apologize."

"I figured as much." Sami boldly studied him from head to toe. "What, no peace offering?"

This was better than he'd hoped for. She was cool, but at least she was speaking to him. "I was going to bring you roses but I figured the thorns would probably hurt when you flogged me with the bouquet.''

"It's a tempting idea." In the days that had passed since she'd broken down and wept so bitterly, Sami had had lots of time to think. There was no easy answer to her dilemma, nor was there anything she could do to change the past. One consolation she could make, though, was to treat Clay with civility whenever she encountered him. She figured she did owe him that much for old times' sake. She wasn't, however, about to let him step back into her life.

Clay glanced past her. "Aren't you going to ask me in?"

"I hadn't planned on it, no."

He shrugged. "In that case, have you heard from your sister?"

"No. Sorry."

"Then I guess I'll be going."

Sami had just opened her mouth to bid him goodbye when she heard a child's shrill wail coming from the back of the house. *Jess!* Forgetting everything but the fact that her son needed her, she wheeled and ran toward the sound of the distress.

Throwing open the rear screen door, she dashed off the porch to where Jess sat in the middle of the sidewalk, holding his scraped knee and caterwauling unmercifully.

"What is it, honey?" She crouched next to him. "I'm here. Tell me what happened."

Teary-eyed, the child pointed to his reddened knee. "I fall down. Owie." He sniffled, apparently pacified now that he had Sami's undivided attention, and held out his arms to her to be picked up.

She straightened and started to bend down for the boy, her mouth falling open as Clay stepped between them and scooped him up in one smooth motion. Even more shocking was the fact that Jess didn't object.

She bristled. "Where did you come from?"

"The front porch. Remember?"

"I know that, I just meant . . . Oh, never mind." Holding open the screen door, she let Clay and Jess precede her into the kitchen. "Set him on that chair, and I'll get some disinfectant and a bandage."

Jess had begun to whimper once again. As she made her way to the medicine cabinet in the bathroom, Sami heard Clay murmuring words of encouragement. Permitting a nurturing attitude like that would never do if she meant to keep the two apart, she decided. Clay wasn't even supposed to be in the vicinity, let alone kneeling in her kitchen, comforting his young son.

Sami's heart raced with guilt and fear. *His son.* No matter how many times she denied it, the truth was, Clay had a paternal right to the boy.

Her jaw set, her strongly protective instincts taking over her heart in a mighty surge of stubborn resolve. Right or wrong, she was going to get that man out of her house and out of her life at once. She'd simply thank him for his kindness and escort him to the door. Immediately. Without argument.

Hurrying back into the kitchen, a box of colorful adhesive bandages in one hand, peroxide and a washcloth in the other, she was surprised to hear Jess giggling. Coming to an abrupt halt, she paused long enough to realize Clay was promising the child a trip to the local hamburger stand as a prize for bravery during first-aid treatment.

"That won't be necessary, I'm sure," Sami said, interrupting and edging Clay out of the way so she could take his place. "Jess is always good about things like this, aren't you, honey?"

The little boy hung his head and stuck out his lower lip in a theatrical pout. "I like cheeseburgers."

"Of course you do. We have them all the time. Remember?"

Clay gave Sami more room to tend to the scrape. "I'm sorry if I encroached on your territory. It just seemed a natural thing to offer him some kind of a reward for good behavior."

"Well, it isn't."

"Oh." He stuffed his hands into the pockets of his slacks. "Then how about just a regular lunch for no special reason? We all have to eat, and it is getting late. I happen to have a fondness for cheeseburgers, too."

Jess cheered and grinned at his mother. "Yeah!"

"No, thanks." Busying herself with the bandaging, Sami put off making eye contact with Clay, assuming that by the time she finally did, he'd have accepted her ultimatum. She was wrong. When she straightened and took the damp rag to the sink to rinse it out, he was studying her as if she were a visitor from another planet.

He scowled. "Why not? What are you afraid of?"

"Don't be silly."

"Then let's get going." He held out his hand to Jess. "The kid and I are starved."

Sami looked down at the old, tattered clothes she'd been wearing to do her cleaning. "No. Besides, I can't go like this. I'm a sight."

"You said it, I didn't," Clay taunted, trying to lift her spirits, clueless as to why she seemed so unwilling to partake in a harmless little outing.

Glancing from one pair of rich brown eyes to the other, Sami sighed. Their poignant stares were making her feel like the meanest mother in history. Eating was a fairly innocuous pastime. Surely there wouldn't be any danger in letting Jess have one meal with his daddy just to salve her conscience, would there?

"All right. You two hang loose while I go throw on a clean pair of jeans and a T-shirt. But no funny stuff, you hear? We go for hamburgers and that's that. Under-stood?''

"Cheeseburgers!" Jess shouted, jumping up and down, apparently instantly healed.

Sami's eyebrows raised and she rolled her eyes. "I stand corrected. Cheeseburgers." Shooting Clay a steely glance that clearly blamed him for disrupting her day, she hurried toward her room to change.

Decorated predominantly in red and white, with multi-colored flashing neon outlining the rounded corners of the facade, the fifties-style hamburger stand on the corner of First and Palm had been Sami's home away from home since even before Jess was old enough to express a prefer-ence.

The place was casual, colorful and unpretentious, and the minute you opened the door the food smelled so heavenly you couldn't help but be famished. Besides, not having to cook all the time gave her more free hours to devote to her work, and she made sure Jess got plenty of fresh fruit and vegetables at his other meals.

This time, however, she found herself acting as if the choice of a cheeseburger and soda was going to instantly ruin his health.

"No fries," she said aside to Clay. "He'll never be able to eat them all, and they're not that good for him, any-way."

"Potatoes?" Clay regarded her with undisguised amuse-ment. "It's a vegetable, Sami."

"But fried."

"Oh, excuse me."

She scowled up at him. "No need to get sarcastic."

Chuckling, Clay reached down, lifted Jess in his arms and held him up so he could see over the counter. "Okay, kid, tell your uncle Clay. What'll it be? Still want a cheese-burger?''

"Yeah!" The child was grinning broadly while holding tight to Clay's neck.

"Milk to drink?"

The pause was extremely short, as Sami knew it would be. "Soda!"

"Okay, this time," Clay told him, "but you have to drink lots of milk if you want to grow up to be big and strong like me."

Jess seemed to contemplate the suggestion. "Milk's good, too."

"Right. I'll have the same. And we'll share a large order of fries." He turned to Sami. "What would you like?"

"I'm not very hungry." Unfortunately, the innocent statement had come out sounding like she was simply being difficult for the sake of argument. In reality, being around Clay and watching him relate so well to Jess had all but killed her usually hearty appetite.

Clay smiled at the child in his arms. "Your mom's being a real pill today, kid. Is she always like this?" He chuckled at the confused look on the boy's cherubic face. "Never mind. We'll just get a few extra burgers and she can eat whatever she wants. Okay?"

"Okay," Jess said.

Clay leaned over and passed him to Sami while he paid for their lunch. As soon as she set Jess on the floor, he was off at a run for the door to the enclosed play yard the restaurant had geared especially to its preschool customers.

Pocketing his change, Clay looked at Sami while he waited for the counter girl to load their tray. "I see you never feed the kid here," he taunted. "He obviously has no idea where the toys are or how to get to them."

"I never said we didn't eat here," she countered.

"Oh? I could have sworn you were acting as if I was trying to poison your son with dreaded fast food."

"I just don't like to be bullied."

"Bullied? Samantha, this is a *treat*, not a prison sentence. Lighten up, will you?"

She had to admit he did have a valid point. "Sorry."

"Apology accepted." Lifting the full tray, Clay nodded toward a booth next to the broad window that looked out onto the play yard where Jess was busily climbing on a red plastic structure. The object resembled a sandbox, except that its base was filled with multicolored balls instead of sand.

"Over there looks good," Clay said. "Then, if our little friend gets bored he can leave us and we can still keep an eye on him."

Sami followed. What amazed her the most was the naturalness of Clay's actions with regard to Jess. It was as if the man had been rehearsing for fatherhood all his life and had effortlessly stepped into the role the moment he had the chance.

When she caught Jess's eye, crooked her index finger and signaled through the window, he came immediately, clambering over her lap to stand on the plastic seat where he could make a grab for the fries.

Seated across the table, Clay reached out and moved them away. "Sit down politely and I'll give you some."

Jess pouted but did as he was told.

"He's only a little over two years old," Sami said, miffed.

"And at what age did you begin using good manners?"

"I don't remember."

"Well, I do," he said, smiling. "I was six, so you couldn't have been much older than Jess is right now. My mother and yours got together to throw me a surprise birthday party and your mom brought you along." As he reminisced, he was unwrapping Jess's cheeseburger and placing it beside a handful of fries on the yellow waxed-paper wrapper in front of him. "Okay, kid, dig in."

"I don't remember much," Sami said, trying to picture the long-past event. All she could recall was a vague aura of excitement and the feeling that the other children were much older than she was.

"You had on a pink dress, all ruffles and bows, and I remember being mortified at having a *girl* at my party. Especially such a tiny one." He laughed out loud.

"Was I awful?" Sami accepted the hamburger he handed her and took a bite without thinking.

"No. Not at all. You were darned cute. Of course, at the time, I wasn't old enough to appreciate any female. The thing is, I have this vivid image of you, shyly eating your serving of cake and ice cream and putting us boys to shame with your ladylike table manners."

"Me?" Sami blushed.

Clay laughed again, quiet and low. "Yes, you. Hard to believe, isn't it?"

"The part that's hard to believe is that you'd actually remember such a minor thing for so long."

"I remember everything I ever knew about you," he said softly.

She chose to overlook the overt tribute. "Children were raised differently in my parents' day. I suppose they expected a lot of me."

"Probably not nearly as much as you expected of yourself." Clay extended the cardboard tray of french fries, then withdrew it when Sami shook her head. "I get the feeling you're still far too hard on yourself. There is no perfect parent, you know."

She glanced over at Jess. He was eating his cheeseburger as carefully as he could and watching Clay as if he were God personified. When the man reached for a french fry, the boy mimicked him and did the same. She wouldn't have believed the improvement in Jess's manners if she hadn't witnessed it in person.

"Kids are marvelous little people," Clay said. "You'd be surprised how much they can learn, and how fast, if you just set the rules and give them a chance."

Sami remained silent, unwilling to challenge Clay in front of the boy, who was watching their exchange with undisguised interest. "Are you almost finished?" she asked, when he put the tattered remnants of his cheeseburger down.

"Uh-huh."

She wiped his hands for him. "Then you may go back outside and play for a few minutes."

Jess looked to Clay for the final word. At his nod of permission, the boy slid off the seat, ducked under the edge of the table and hurried to the playground door.

Sami put aside her half-eaten burger and squared her shoulders. "I'd appreciate it if you'd let me take care of Jess's discipline. He'll get confused if he gets too many conflicting directions."

Clay cocked one eyebrow. "And I'm only his uncle by marriage. I take it you disagree with the way I asked him to behave."

"It's not that, exactly."

"Then what is it...exactly?" He popped the last fry into his mouth after offering it to her and having her wave it away impatiently.

"He's *my* son and I'm raising him the way I think best," she said. "I can do it fine alone."

Clay sighed, nodded and began to gather up their trash. "I suppose that's the crux of our whole problem, isn't it? You always wanted to do things on your own, and nothing's changed. There's no place in your life for me, is there, Samantha?"

Answering him was harder than she'd imagined. "No."

"I wish I could be more like you." Clay rose and headed for the waste receptacle with their tray. She followed. "I need someone in my life who'll always be there for me," he said. "Somebody who cares about me for myself, not just because I happen to run a successful business and drive an expensive car."

"Vicki," Sami murmured, knowing all too well her sister's penchant for wealth and ease of living.

Clay nodded as he dumped the wastepaper and empty cups. "Yeah, Vicki. I wish..." Turning, he looked over his shoulder, expecting to find Sami still standing nearby. Instead, he saw her entering the play yard to retrieve Jess.

That was some special little boy, Clay thought. But then, he had a pretty phenomenal mother, didn't he? The hardest part was thinking about the two of them without including the man who was Jess's father.

As Clay started after them, he wondered if he'd ever be able to calmly accept the idea that Sami had loved another man enough to bear his child. Somehow, he doubted it.

The drive back to Sami's was pretty peaceful once Jess unwound enough to nod off to sleep.

"He's used to an afternoon nap, even though he objects every time I put him down," she remarked in passing.

"I figured as much." He pulled into her driveway and braked slowly to keep from waking the sleepy little boy. "Want me to help you carry him up to bed?"

"I can manage."

Clay found himself growing impatient with her constant inferences that he was questioning her capabilities. "I know you can. What I was offering was to *help* you. That's all."

"You can bring the car seat if you want," Sami said, leaning over to unfasten the belt around Jess.

Clay complied and followed her to the door, standing out of the way while she balanced her sleeping son on one hip and unlocked the house. He would have volunteered to wield the key for her, but he figured she would probably bite his head off if he said a word.

She gestured toward the interior. "Just set the seat on the floor in the entry. I'll put it back in my car later."

Watching her climb the stairs to the bedrooms, he lowered the car seat into the corner by the staircase and waited. His sensible side told him he should leave before she returned. Another, more primitive, part of his psyche insisted he stay. The basic instinct won.

Sami seemed surprised to see him standing there when she came back down the stairs.

"I suppose I should get going," Clay said, not sounding at all convincing, "but I thought maybe we could talk a little more freely now that we're alone."

"About what?" Sami hated the way her words kept coming out, all hard and unfriendly, yet there was some built-in defense mechanism in her that kept triggering dire warnings and insisting she remain standoffish.

The dejected expression on his face helped her reconsider. "Never mind. Since you're still here, how about some cold lemonade?"

"Iced tea sounds better," he said, making his way past her quickly, before she could change her mind. "I remember your lemonade."

Sami chuckled. "I was ten years old when I made the infamous batch you're talking about, Clay. I know you're supposed to sweeten it now."

"That's bound to be an improvement."

She started for the kitchen. "I never claimed to be Julia Child. Want to come along and count the scoops of sugar to be sure it's safe to drink this time?"

"Okay." Relieved to have something to do besides stand around and risk giving her time to think of a good reason to banish him, he followed her across the narrow hallway and into the long-ago-remodeled, oak-and-copper kitchen, looking around while keeping a discreet distance.

Sami placed fresh lemons, a knife and a glass citrus press on the tile counter, stepped away and pointed. "Go for it. You squeeze, and I'll measure."

She watched him take up the task with a smile. If she'd known ahead of time how twisting the lemon halves on the spindle would make the muscles in his arms bulge and draw her attention to the fine, dark hairs on his bared forearms, she never would have asked him to help. She of all people should have known better. Allowing herself to note exciting details of Clay's body was about as smart as playing volleyball in the fast lane of the freeway at rush hour.

Forcing her gaze away, she offered some small talk as a distraction. "We pretty well covered the latest changes in my newspaper career at lunch. How are you doing these days?"

"Okay. I'd be a lot better off if I could find your sister, though," Clay said, slicing cleanly through another lemon and releasing a burst of tangy citrus aroma. "I really need that piece of property she owns on Sycamore for my latest shopping center."

"Have you built a lot of those? I thought you were mostly into apartments and condos."

"I was, back before you went north. Since then, I've switched to bigger projects. The financing is much more complicated but the profits are also better—providing all the loose ends can be tied together." He paused. "You know, when I get involved in a mess like the one I'm in now, I realize how much I miss swinging a framing hammer, like in the old days."

"Boy, *I* don't."

"Come again?"

She shrugged. "Oh, nothing. I started fixing the grape arbor the other day and I'm still sore." Clay had passed her the nearly full squeezer. As she began to empty it into a measuring cup, some of the potent juice got on her hands and she winced. "Ouch."

"Here. Let me see."

"No. It's nothing. Really." She stuck her fingers under the spigot and rinsed them off.

Without hesitation, Clay grasped her wrists, turned her hands palm-up and made a guttural sound when he saw the blisters. "Geez, Sami. You look like you built a three-story house all by yourself. How'd you do this?"

She pulled a silly face. Anything to keep from showing how much his tenderness and genuine concern were affecting her. "The grape arbor. I told you."

"Well, don't do anything like that again. If these blisters got infected you'd be in deep trouble."

"Unless I want this place to fall down around me, I've got to do some things. It's older than I am."

"That old, huh?" He released her when he realized he was enjoying the prolonged contact far too much.

"Shut up, Ellis. You're older than I am, too."

"Only by a few years, although it feels like a dozen, thanks to your sister."

Sami stiffened. "Let's talk about something else, okay? Something safer, like religion or politics?"

"Sure," he said, drying his hands. "Look, while I'm here, why don't I help you fix up the place a little? You know. Like I used to. Maybe I could finish the arbor."

"No way."

"Why not?"

"There's no need. Really."

"Oh, no? Care to show me your blisters again while you repeat that?"

"I just meant—"

"I know. You're perfectly capable of doing everything for yourself, and besides, you don't want to owe me."

Sami rubbed her palms on her shirt and eyed him defensively, cautiously.

"You shouldn't be surprised I can read your mind," Clay said. "I've been doing it for years." He sobered. "At least, in some areas."

"I told you, I really don't want to talk about the past. Why do we always seem to come back to it?"

"Maybe because we haven't been together much since the old days. Sometimes it seems like you don't want me to know anything about you anymore." He leaned against the edge of the kitchen counter and studied her.

Sami looked into the dark depths of his eyes and was instantly transported back to happier times. Once or twice, before Clay and Vicki had gotten married, she'd felt so close to him, so safe, she'd seriously considered sharing tales of the trauma of her teen years. Now she was extremely glad she hadn't. It was bad enough that he thought she'd had Jess out of wedlock, without adding the shame of the genuinely sordid story that was the bane of her early life.

"I just want to do something nice for you," he said. "Is that too hard to understand?"

"I guess not."

"Then let me finish repairing the arbor."

"It's a pretty big job. The uprights are strong but the cross-members are half-rotted away and the old vines get in the way when you're working."

He snorted a chuckle. "Seems like we've already decided I'm an expert about old stuff getting in the way." Heading for the back door, he called over his shoulder, "You finish making the lemonade while I assess the repairs."

"But..." Sami wasn't quite sure when she'd given him permission to go to work on her house, but apparently Clay was convinced she had. And, perhaps, if she were to ask her heart, she would find she'd *wanted* him to believe he was welcome to hang around for a while. Seeing him again was like returning to cheerful, more uncomplicated times.

She sighed. There were even a few blessed moments during their latest hours together when she hadn't felt frightened.

Chapter Four

Putting ice cubes into two tumblers, Sami filled them with the freshly made lemonade and went outside to see what Clay was up to. He'd moved her rickety stepladder beneath the arbor and was halfway up it, his head lost in the tangle of grape leaves.

When he sensed her presence, he descended and accepted the frosty drink she offered. "Thanks. I'm thirsty." The instant he tipped the glass up and swallowed, he began to choke and cough.

Astonished at the violent, unexpected reaction, Sami pressed her fingertips to her lips. She couldn't have been so lost in thought she forgot to sweeten it again, could she? One tiny sip later, she knew she certainly could. And had.

His face contorting, his fist thumping his chest melodramatically, Clay made a dash for the back door. "Sugar. Help!"

Sami was way ahead of him. Grabbing the sugar bowl off the table, she ladled out a heaping spoonful and held it up, eeding him the way she had Jess when he was a baby.

Clay opened his mouth, then closed it slowly, purposefully, around the spoon. Their eyes locked, their breathing
ceased for an instant of recognition. Clay placed his larger
hand over hers to guide it, slipped the spoon out of his
mouth and licked stray granules off his lips.

Transfixed, Sami stared at his sensuous, strong mouth,
the way his tongue moistened it, the way his dark eyes spoke
to her soul in ways she didn't pretend to fathom.

Taking a step closer, still holding her hand with the spoon
in it, he lowered it out of the way. His voice was hoarse, his
body so tense the muscles in his jaw were quivering. "Now
we know the truth," he said breathlessly. "Don't we?"

"What truth?" Her heart supplied plenty of answers, like
We know we're in love and *We know we belong together,* but
she wisely kept those unacceptable opinions to herself.

Clay saved the situation with his ready wit. "We know
you still can't make decent lemonade," he said, purposely
contradicting the actuality he sensed was as plainly written
on his face, in his eyes, as it was in Sami's.

"I guess I did forget the sugar again," she said. "It's all
your fault."

"Mine?" His fingers continued to hold hers, loath to let
go. "Why?"

"Because you distract me and you know it," she admitted, pulling her hand from his grasp. "You always have."

"Is that so bad?"

"For me it is. It's my fault. I shouldn't have let myself
dwell on the past. I don't want to discuss anything about it.
As far as I'm concerned, I intend to forget I even knew you
before you married my sister, and that's all there is to it."

She spun away so he couldn't see the torment in her eyes.
"Put some sugar in the lemonade, Clay. I'm going upstairs
to check on Jess."

Taking up a measuring cup and the sugar canister, he di(
as she'd instructed, watching the sparkling white granule:
spill through the air into the pitcher. Too bad a man couldn'
go back and relive his life once he figured out what he'(
done to screw it up. Given another chance, he hoped h(
would at least be smart enough not to fall in love with on(
sister and marry the other on the rebound.

Upstairs, Sami gazed down at her sleeping son, her con
science doing cartwheels while her heart thumped errati
cally. To her credit, she hadn't tried to fool any of he
friends in the bay area into believing she'd actually give
birth. It was enough to simply switch identities with Vick
when the mother-to-be visited her obstetrician and befor(
she entered the hospital. That way, Sami's name would ap
pear on the birth certificate and there wouldn't be any hang
ups about adoption.

Vicki, always more concerned about herself than anyon(
else, had pitched a royal fit the day the baby was being born

"I *had* to let you talk me into this." Another contractio:
struck and she gasped, doubling up and rolling half onto he
side on the sofa. "Oh, my God."

Sticking with her every waking moment for the past fev
weeks, Sami had been used to her regular tirades, but not t(
the panic she now detected in her younger sister's voice.

She patted Vicki's arm. "It'll be all right. Just do like w
learned in class. Come on, breathe."

"*You* breathe," Vicki had shot back. "I'm busy bein;
turned inside out." She moaned, the pitch climbing.

"Was that another pain?" Sami glanced at her wris'
watch when Vicki nodded. "Looks like they're getting close
together. We'd better start for the hospital." Reaching fo
Vicki's overnight bag, she held out her free hand. "Gra
hold. I'll help you up."

The mother-to-be waved her off till the contraction had ceased, then accepted the offer of assistance. "I feel like a damn beached whale being run over by a convoy of fully loaded semitrucks," she said with a grimace. "My hair's a mess, I haven't had my nails properly done in weeks, there are ugly stretch marks all over my stomach, and you're so damn upbeat and capable I could puke."

"You're doing the right thing, honey. The good thing."

"Hah! The only *good thing* to come out of all this is the best pair of boobs I've ever had and I suppose those will disappear as soon as I get rid of the freeloader down here." She patted her distended abdomen. "God, I wish this was over."

"Me, too," Sami said, assisting her out the door and into the apartment elevator. "How are you doing?"

"Oh, just peachy."

Sami smiled to hide her concern for her sister's welfare. "Good. I have a taxi waiting."

"Thank heavens. After the way my week has gone so far, I figured you'd probably expect me to ride the trolley!"

Sami chuckled. "That's better. Put some humor into it. Might as well. It'll probably be a long night."

"For me, anyway," Vicki cracked back. "I sure wish we could really become each other instead of only pretending. I don't deserve to go through all this and then have you take home the prize. Hell, you probably won't even work up a good sweat."

But Sami had. Staying with her sister all through labor, coaching her, cajoling her, crying, praying, laughing and finally rejoicing when the baby was born, well and healthy, Sami felt that she, too, had experienced the miracle first-hand. And she was as totally exhausted as Vicki.

Best of all, their ruse had worked without a hitch. The colorful names Vicki had called her during the labor and delivery ordeal had had nothing to do with reality. As far as the authorities knew, Samantha Louise Adamson had entered the hospital, borne a son and named him Jess. Where the records asked for the name of the father, a clerk had simply typed, "Declines to state," and left it at that.

When Jess was tiny, Sami's colleagues had treated him as part of their extended family. She could easily have stayed in San Francisco and carried on as always, if she hadn't been so worried that someone might eventually question the fact she'd never been pregnant and wonder too much about how she came to be the boy's parent of record. Besides, something about Redlands had drawn her back. It was home. Safe. Comfortable.

Never in a million years would she have imagined that one day she, Jess and Clay would all be together under one roof like a real family. The whole scenario was straight out of her wildest fantasies.

And extremely dangerous, she added. Fantasies were for suckers, not sensible career women with clanking, rattling family skeletons hidden in every blessed closet in the house.

While Jess slept, she decided she'd change into her old clothes again and help Clay finish the arbor, then thank him kindly and send him on his way. No, it wasn't what she honestly wanted to do, but it was what she was *going* to do. Nobody, not even his real father, was going to take her son away from her while she had an ounce of fight left in her body or a trace of determination clinging to her spirit.

She'd been beaten down before, more than once, and had refused to give up. This time was no different. Not even with her newly rekindled love for Clay Ellis as part of the equation.

* * *

"Hand me another one of those stringers I cut," Clay called down to her from his precarious perch atop the arbor.

Sami turned the long, narrow board on end and passed it up through the gnarled tangle of vines, holding it as steady as she could till he took it from her. "Anything else?"

"No. I'm about done. Good thing, too. I'm cooking, up here in the sun." He paused long enough to strip off his shirt, then tossed it down to her. "Catch."

Without thinking, Sami reached out and snagged the fluttering garment. The moment she felt the warm fabric in her hands she was instantly sorry she had caught it. His encompassing radiance was so potent even the simple shirt retained his aura, the magnetism that was exclusively Clay's.

Clearly, all her senses were becoming more and more heightened the longer he remained in her proximity. Every look carried hidden messages directly to her heart; every word he spoke sent shivery tingles racing up her spine. Just as he'd stepped so easily into the role of parent, he was now reentering the rest of her life as if he'd never left. That would never do.

Sami carefully folded the light blue polo shirt, hugging the small bundle to her breast when she was done and trying to decide what to do next. Clay's handy excuse that he needed to locate Vicki kept popping up in their conversations. All right. If that was true, then he should be satisfied to drop back out of her life once he'd accomplished his stated goal.

Of course, it was foolhardy to assume Vicki would be able or willing to keep their secret if she was given the opportunity to speak at any length with her ex-husband. It wasn't her nature to keep confidences very well. Therefore, Sami had come up with a safer solution. As soon as Clay descended, she tried to present it to him.

"I have a great idea," she said, averting her gaze to keep from staring at the glistening perspiration highlighting his hard-muscled upper torso.

He bent over to turn on a garden hose and ran cool water over his neck, head and arms. "Unless it includes conjuring up a swimming pool in the next few minutes, count me out."

Turning off the water, he straightened and raked his dark, thick hair straight back with his fingers, letting the excess water trickle down his back. "*Boy,* it's hot today."

"You're the one who insisted you had to charge out here and hammer something," she reminded him. "Are you done?"

Clay was brushing off his slacks and wishing he'd worn a pair of tougher jeans. "I've accomplished about as much as we can hope for without tearing the whole structure down and starting over, yes."

He straightened, drawing the back of his forearm across his damp forehead. "How about some cold lemonade while I sit out here for a few minutes and cool off?"

"Okay. Park yourself under a tree. I'll be right back."

Sami hurried, but by the time she returned with two glasses of the now-sweetened beverage, Clay had lain down on the grass, his hands laced behind his head and his eyes closed.

Figuring there was no way he could have actually nodded off so quickly, she stood above him and dribbled a few drops of his icy drink onto the center of his chest. Her aim was excellent.

"Ow! Why you..."

Sami was giggling. "Your drink, sir?"

"I'd rather have mine in a glass," Clay said, levering himself slowly into a sitting position. "But if you want to sip yours off my chest, I suggest you allow me to take a shower first."

His smile was languid, his eyes only half-open, and Sami felt herself begin to blush from her toes to the roots of her hair. Quickly, she shoved one of the still full glasses into his hand and backed away.

Clay laughed and shook his head. "You know, for a woman who's had a child, you sure are naive. Didn't you learn not to be so bashful when you lived in San Francisco? I understand that's a pretty liberal city."

"Where a person lives has nothing to do with it," Sami said. "We are what we are." She paused. "Speaking of which, you never listened to my idea."

"Okay." Leaning back and setting aside his drink after chug-a-lugging half of it, he looked up at her. "Go ahead. Shoot. I'm paying attention."

"It's about Vicki," Sami said, instantly warming to her subject. "All you have to do is tell me exactly what it is you need her to do or sign or whatever, and I'll be your messenger. Sort of a go-between."

His eyes narrowed again. "I thought you said you didn't know where she was."

"Well, I . . ." In her enthusiasm for the plan, she hadn't counted on Clay getting technical about it.

"Which is it, Samantha? Do you or don't you?"

"I may. That's not the point."

"It's *exactly* the point. How could you go on lying to me like that?"

"Don't push me, Clay. I'm offering to do you a favor."

"You'll be doing us all a favor if you cut the crap and start leveling with me. Where is your sister?"

She set her jaw, her lips pressed into a thin line.

Clay was on his feet in one fluid motion, advancing on her. "Where is she, Sami? You're not doing her any good by hiding her. I'm willing to pay more than fair market value for the property. It's a better deal than she'd get from anyone else."

"Then why not let me carry that message to her? Why is it so important that *you* be the one to make the offer?" Considering his imposing size and the nearness of his bared chest, she thought she was doing extremely well to keep the nervous quaver solely in her stomach and out of her voice.

"Because of the kind of person Vicki is," he said. "She won't believe my story unless I lay out all the details for her and convince her she's getting the best of me."

"I can do that."

He shot her a stormy glance. "Not unless I tell you a lot more about my personal finances than I care to."

Sami wondered if there was anything he could have said right then that would have hurt her more. Apparently, Clay felt Vicki still came first. Did having once been married do that to a person's priorities? she wondered. Or was it more a case of him believing his ex-wife deserved his confidence while Sami did not?

"I see," she said flatly.

Clay reached out and grasped her shoulders. "No, you don't see. I have my pride, too, Sami. When things don't go well for me I always wind up thinking about how disappointed you'd be if you knew." His grip tightened.

Once again, the familiar dread of being physically restrained began to take control of her mind, bringing with it the awful memories she wanted so desperately to be rid of. It was difficult to stand her ground while Clay's strong fingers continued to hold her prisoner, but for once she succeeded.

Taking deep, calming breaths, Sami managed to talk herself out of trying to escape by reminding herself that it was her old friend, Clay, holding on to her and he would never intentionally do her any harm. The urge to twist away and flee was still present, just not quite so irrationally out-of-control as before.

"I could never be disappointed in you," she said. The shaky timbre of her voice served as unspoken contradiction.

"Oh, no? What about at the wedding?"

He didn't need to be precise about which blessed event he meant. As far as Sami was concerned, there was only one wedding in her life—Clay and Vicki's. Misty-eyed, she turned her face away.

"I didn't mean to hurt you, then or ever," he said. "Damn it, I didn't intend to hurt anyone. Honest to God, I thought I was doing the right thing."

"I know you did. I tried to warn you, but..." Her voice broke.

"Don't you know why I wouldn't listen?"

She shook her head in the negative.

"I was still smarting from the way you'd dumped me. Think about it. The woman who refuses to marry me, then runs as far and as fast as she can, suddenly shows up hours before my wedding and begins telling me I shouldn't marry my chosen bride because she'd not *good* enough for me. Hell, Sami, put yourself in my place. What would you have done?"

"I don't know."

Clay nodded somberly. "I'd made a commitment to your sister. I thought we were in love. In a way, I guess we were. I loved the idea of finally finding someone like you, and Vicki loved the balance in my bank account."

"I'm really sorry. I did want you to be happy."

One tear slid silently down her cheek. Clay brushed it aside with his thumb, returning his caress to Sami's shoulders. "Then why did you leave me?"

Incredulous, she looked up at him. "Don't you get it? I *expected* you to find someone else. I wanted you to. I just hadn't counted on it being my own sister."

He dropped his hands. "You're kidding." Shock over-
came him; his jaw slackened.

"No. I'm totally serious."

Outrage began to take over. "You mean, *I'm* the reason
you changed jobs and put all that distance between us? You
thought you were helping me?"

"Yes." She sniffled. "Is that so strange?"

"Strange? It's idiotic!" Pacing away, he wheeled back to
face her. "I thought you'd left because you'd put your career first. Instead, you pull a stupid stunt like that."

"Thanks a heap!"

"Oh, don't thank *me*," Clay shouted. "I'm the one who
should be grateful. Not only did I get a rotten marriage and
divorce out of the deal, I got to see what both you and your
sister are really like."

"Stop it!" Sami clamped her palms over her ears, but she
could still hear his harsh words echoing inside her head. "I
never did anything bad to you," she insisted.

"Oh, no? How about getting pregnant? That's sure not
one of the top ten on my list of wonderful surprises."

The moment the ruthless observation was out of his
mouth he regretted it. Just because his masculine pride had
been bruised, he had no right to take his anger out on her.
The anguish reflected in her eyes tied his gut in knots. Worse
was the hard, unfeeling look that quickly took the place of
her pain.

Clay reached out a hand to her. "Sami, I'm sorry. I
shouldn't have said that."

Back in total control, thanks to his bluntness, she
straightened her spine and looked directly into his face while
brushing aside the last of her sparse tears. "I'm glad you
did. I think you should go now. I've had quite enough fun
for one afternoon."

"Can I call you?"

"What for?"

None of the answers Clay came up with were remotely adequate, so he simply picked up his discarded shirt and brushed past her on his way through the house to his car.

Standing alone in the dappled shade of the arbor, Sami listened carefully till she heard his car start up and drive away. Then, all the rigidity seemed to leave her body in a rush. Her shoulders slumped, and she sighed deeply and noisily.

What she really wanted to do at that moment was let herself go completely and cry buckets, she decided, but try as she might, her mind and body refused to cooperate.

Instead of the roiling emotions she'd expected, Sami realized she was feeling very little, sort of like when her foot went to sleep and she hardly knew it was still there.

And apparently her heart was similarly numb, along with the rest of her. Once again she'd paid dearly for her subterfuge about Jess; only this time the price was the highest ever—Clay's respect.

"But Jess is worth it," she muttered, consciously forcing her feet to take one step after another toward the house. Every bit of that statement was true. Jess was her life. And she loved him more than anything or anyone on earth. So why was she feeling as if her best friend had just died and left her so sorrowful and bereft she could hardly function?

Making a disgusted face at herself in the glass of the back door, she entered the kitchen. The half-full lemonade pitcher still sat on the counter, the sugar canister beside it where Clay had left it.

Those two inanimate objects were a perfect example of exactly what her existence was like, she mused, pausing to visualize the comparison. The life she'd chosen was like unsweetened lemonade...healthy, but nevertheless lacking an essential ingredient to make it more palatable, more enjoyable.

Sighing, she slid the pitcher into the refrigerator. Maybe what she needed to do was look around for somebody—other than her old flame—who could bring back the sweetness to her life. The trouble was, she couldn't picture anyone doing that but Clay Ellis.

Chapter Five

There were a lot of confusing emotions cluttering up Clay's consciousness as he drove home to Victorville that evening. The most distressing was the idea his thoughtless outburst had caused Sami unnecessary grief. What was wrong with them, anyway? Why did they wind up quarreling every time they were together?

He sighed. In his deepest heart, he knew he cared for Sami, probably more than ever, and the last thing he wanted to do was fight with her. Yet they seemed always on edge, always at each other's throats.

Then, there was the matter of Vicki. Surely Sami must have a better reason than mere sibling protectiveness for refusing to tell him where her sister was. Hell, the way she was acting, you would think Vicki was a wanted fugitive or something.

Clay's heart skipped several beats. Could it be? Vicki was always wild and ran with a pretty fast crowd, so he supposed anything was possible, given the right set of circumstances. But would Sami break the law to protect her? People didn't come any more honest than Samantha Adamson. Surely she wouldn't set aside her high moral principles for her sister's sake, would she?

The idea gained credence and momentum as he mulled it over. Sami, as the oldest, had always mothered and protected Vicki, even when they were both still children. There was no reason to suppose she'd stopped just because they'd grown up. Besides, as Vicki's legal guardian for eight years, she'd undoubtedly formed the habit of taking responsibility. If Vicki were in a jam now, Sami would naturally protect her.

Clay's gut wrenched. Sami could get herself in big trouble going out on a limb for her sister like that. And if she put herself in serious jeopardy, what would become of Jess? Poor little guy. Didn't Sami realize the boy should come first in her priorities?

"Enough," he said, the harshly spoken expression of disgust echoing inside his speeding car. He reached for his cellular phone, punched in his office number and listened to the ringing. Instead of the answering-machine message he'd expected, his secretary answered.

"Judith? This is Clay. What are you doing there on the weekend?"

"Working," she said matter-of-factly. "*Somebody* has to show up around here once in a while to hold this business together."

Clay chuckled, picturing her familiar rounded face, short, wavy brown hair, sprightly manner and the cynical smile he knew she was displaying as she chided him. The middle-aged woman was irreplaceable and they'd long ago developed the casual rapport and mutual respect that made working together easy and pleasant.

"I'm still doing fieldwork," he told her.

"Right. So tell me. Did you find your ex-wife?"

"Not yet. That's why I'm calling. I want you to get hold of Dick Rasmussen and set up a meeting as soon as possible."

"I thought you weren't going to need private investigators. What happened to asking your wife's sister for help?"

"That didn't work out. Sami swore she didn't know anything about Vicki." He recalled their quarrel beneath the arbor. "Only she let it slip that she could deliver a message for me. That's pretty hard to do if you don't know where a person is."

"Damned near impossible," Judith said. "While I have you on the line, Parker wants to see you about the anchor stores for the mall getting nervous because of the delays, the environmentalists are screaming about kangaroo-rat habitat being destroyed, and Alvarez wants to know when he can let his crew start grading." She paused for a breath. "And—"

"Rasmussen first. Call him at home if you have to," Clay said. "Once he locates Vicki for me, half my problems will be solved."

"But what should I tell the Indians?"

"The *what?*"

"I was trying to explain. A delegation of local Native Americans wants to talk to you about the possibility there may be an ancient burial ground located within the boundaries of our Sycamore development."

Clay wished he had an aspirin. Make that two. "Okay. We might as well put the delay to good use. Get an archaeologist from the university and send him out in the field with their people. Tell them to dig to their hearts' content and offer to hire whatever help they say they need. And make sure Parker doesn't blab to the anchors. The last thing we need is our big-name stores backing out because of this."

"Right. Anything else?"

"Yes. Call Alvarez, apologize and tell him it'll probably be at least a month before we can break ground."

"What about the rat people?"

"Well put," Clay said, hearing the wry humor coloring her voice. "Tell them . . . Never mind. I'll tell them myself when I've seen the latest surveys. Hopefully, our furry little k-rat population has packed its bags and headed for the hills."

"Where can I contact you?" Judith asked.

"For the next two hours, in my car. After that I'm going to be at home trying to get some sleep so I'll be lucid enough to figure out whether my ex-wife is on the lam."

"I beg your pardon?"

"You heard me."

"I'll hurry with Dick Rasmussen. Sounds like you really do need him."

"Damned if I know," Clay said. "To tell you the truth, I hope I'm wasting my money."

It was early the next morning before Clay heard from Judith. The sun was just starting to crest the ridge of mountains that ringed the broad valley. Planning to take advantage of the natural terrain, he'd built his house up a draw so it was shaded almost till noon. In the high desert that helped a lot, especially in the summer.

He rubbed his hand across the stubble on his chin as he answered the telephone in the kitchen. Wonderful aromas wafted from the hot coffee dripping through the coffee-maker suspended beneath the unadorned ash cabinets. Across the room on the stark, white counter, a box of yesterday's donuts sat waiting for the coffee to finish brewing.

"Hello?"

"Good morning," Judith said. "I hope you're awake, because Rasmussen should be there in about ten minutes."

"Awake and even dressed, thanks. Anything else?"

"Nothing that won't keep. I've handled the Native Americans to their satisfaction, and the rat people have been strangely quiet, considering. How did you sleep?"

Clay sighed. "Fine." He gazed out the window at the beige-and-gray rock cliffs rising behind the house. Higher up, against the clear blue sky, a hawk circled effortlessly in the updrafts from the valley floor.

"Did you tell Dick what I wanted?"

"I thought you could do that better than I could. I just mentioned that you were a little strung out by all that's happened lately and could use rescuing."

"It's not quite that bad." Clay pulled on the coiled phone cord, stretching it enough to allow him to reach the box of donuts. Sami would have a fit if she saw what he intended to eat for breakfast, wouldn't she? he mused, thanking his secretary for her prompt action and bidding her goodbye.

He bit into a slightly stale sugared donut and smiled. Here he was, miles from Redlands, and he was still thinking about Sami all the time. Pouring a large mug of coffee, he carried his makeshift breakfast into the den, pushed aside a stack of papers on the desk, moved several files off the seat of the leather swivel chair and seated himself in it. Propping the heels of his running shoes on the desk top, he leaned back and sipped his coffee.

While the rest of the house was spotless, thanks to a biweekly cleaning by a professional service, his den was sacrosanct, which was another way of saying unmercifully cluttered. Clay liked it that way. The cleaning crew had straightened up his desk only once before and it had taken him weeks to find everything they'd moved. After that, he'd made the cozy, officelike room off-limits.

Two donuts and another cup of coffee later, Clay heard a knock and went to answer the door, smiling as he greeted his old friend. As usual, the affable private investigator looked like an out-of-shape, middle-aged football fan who spent most weekends propped in front of a TV, guzzling beer and overdosing on pizza. Clay knew the man was proud of his non-threatening image and carefully cultivated it by means of his slightly worn clothing, casual demeanor and shadow of a beard.

He grinned wider as they shook hands. "Hello, Dick. You look half-shot-down."

"Thanks." Rasmussen chuckled. "I aim to please. Judith said you were desperate. What's the problem?"

Clay offered him a cup of coffee, refreshed his own, then led the way back into the den. By the time he'd related the details of all his recent encounters with Sami—minus the part about the kissing—Rasmussen was shaking his head.

"So what do you need me for? You can look in a telephone book or check tax records as well as I can."

"I've done that." Clay set his mug on one corner of the desk, got to his feet and began to pace. "All the regular avenues are dead ends. Mainly, I want you to find out if Sami is placing herself in jeopardy by protecting her sister."

"You actually think the law is after your ex?"

"Maybe. I can't imagine any other reason why Sami would refuse to help me."

"Jealousy?"

Clay shook his head. "No. She's not that kind of person." Approaching, he sat down again nearer the detective and lowered his voice even though they were alone. "Another thing. I want you to contact the hospitals in the San Francisco area and find out when Samantha Louise Adamson gave birth and who the baby's father is."

"Does this have anything to do with finding Vicki?"

"No," Clay said. "That particular information is just for me."

"You're sure it happened in the Bay area?" Rasmussen was taking notes on a pocket pad.

"Yes. A little over two years ago. The child was—is—a boy."

"You've seen him?"

"By accident." Leaning closer, his elbows resting on his knees, Clay clasped his hands together. "I think Sami was ashamed she'd gotten pregnant and didn't want me to know." He looked up at his companion and smiled. "He's one great kid, I tell you."

"Are you and his mother an item? That why you want to know about the father?"

Clay took a deep breath and released it noisily. "No. Sami swears she hates the idea of marriage. Beats the hell out of me why, though. She's a great mother. A little permissive, but I guess that's to be expected since her parents both died when she was just a kid."

"How long have I got?" the detective asked, tucking the notepad into his pocket.

"I want the information yesterday."

Rising, Dick Rasmussen held out his hand and shook his employer's. "That's what I was afraid of."

Sami had tried for days to reach her sister by phone and had no luck whatsoever in spite of leaving repeated messages on the answering machine. Gazing fondly at Jess as he played with a red plastic fire engine in the middle of the rug in her home office, she thought briefly about trying to pay Vicki a visit, then dismissed the offbeat idea as crazy.

The few times she had taken Jess to see his birth mother, Vicki had acted as if their presence was a terrible imposition. Now that she was living and traveling with Mac McCall, a successful rock musician, the only way Sami had managed to keep track of her was to follow his band's concert schedule.

The SinSeers were back in the Inland Empire at present, playing a week-long gig at the Orange Show Grounds. Vicki should have been at the estate in Diamond Bar that she and Mac used as their home base. If so, that meant the only reason she hadn't responded to her telephone messages was because she didn't want to.

Sami sighed. Oh, well. Perhaps it was for the best that Vicki chose to distance herself from Jess. It was too bad the little boy wouldn't have a chance to get to know his aunt, but at least that way he wouldn't be continually disappointed by her, either.

Jess looked up from his play. "Mama? You cryin'?"

"No, honey. Not really." Sami crouched down and held out her arms, and he came running to her for a hug. "I just got something in my eye."

"It hurts?"

"Only a little."

A grin spread across the toddler's face, his eyes alight with an idea. "Uncle Clay can fix you." He held up his knee for inspection. "He fixed me. See?"

The small bandage was already coming loose, so Sami lifted one end and pulled it back. "You're right." She kissed his knee above the scrape. "All better."

The teary-eyed look that Jess had mentioned before grew more noticeable as she recalled how perfect, how ideal, man and boy had looked together. If only Jess's simple logic were correct. If only Clay *could* fix everything.

Jess stood on tiptoe to clasp her tightly around the neck. "Don't cry, Mama."

She straightened with the loving little boy in her arms and balanced his weight on one hip. "I'm fine, honey. Your hugs make me feel much better. I'll be just fine. I promise."

Oh, Clay, why did you have to come back into my life? she thought. *And how in heaven's name am I going to get you out again?*

Carrying Jess with her because she didn't want to let him go, she made her way to the desk, picked up the telephone and dialed her sister's number once again.

The answering machine took the call, with the dulcet tones of Mac's stage voice making Sami's skin crawl. This time, she decided to drop all pretense of genteel formality and tell it like it was.

"Vicki. It's me, Sami," she said as soon as the signal tone sounded. "Your sister. Remember? I *have* to talk to you. It's a matter of life or death. Really. Call me, please. This is the fourth or fifth message I've left and—" Another beep cut her off and she slammed the receiver down in disgust.

"Oh, Jess, what am I going to do?" she muttered.

"Go outside and play!" he answered immediately, squirming loose from her possessive embrace and running out the door. She heard his footsteps slow as he negotiated the staircase, then speed up again on his way across the hall and through the kitchen. The screen door slammed.

"Go out and play. Sure," Sami grumbled. "Boy, do I wish adult life was that simple."

Jess was tucked into bed for the night and Sami was seated at her computer terminal, trying to put an interesting spin on a boring story about a Dutch elm disease infestation in local trees, when the telephone rang. Snatching it up on the first ring, she was sure it had to be Vicki calling her back as requested.

"Hello! It's about time."

"Time for what?" Clay asked.

"Oh. It's you."

"Well, don't get too enthusiastic. I might think you and I are still friends."

"We are."

"Oh, really?"

"What's that supposed to mean?" She was dead tired and her powers of concentration were nil, thanks to him. The last thing she needed to hear was more of his uncalled-for sarcasm.

"I just talked to a buddy of mine."

"Good for you. With your attitude, I'm surprised you have any buddies left."

"Thanks for the vote of confidence. Aren't you going to ask what he told me?"

Sami held her breath, afraid Clay had located Vicki and found out the truth about Jess. "Not really."

"Well, I'll tell you, anyway. He's been in touch with the hall of records in San Francisco."

Sami's stomach churned, bitter bile rising in her throat. "So?"

"So, it seems a certain Ms. Samantha Louise Adamson gave birth to a baby boy a couple of years ago."

"*That* shouldn't have come as a surprise. You've met him."

Clay paused, censoring his more livid thoughts before speaking. "It seems Ms. Adamson declined to state just who the father of her child was."

"That's her prerogative."

"But why? Unless, of course, she really had no idea who the lucky guy was." He was baiting her, hoping she'd co-operate. Since she'd already admitted she'd loved Jess's father, of course she knew exactly who he was.

Sami had to exert an enormous amount of willpower to keep from shouting at him to mind his own business.

"Whoever he is," Clay went on, "he should help you support Jess. The selfish bastard deserves to pay for his mistakes, too."

"What makes you think Jess was a mistake?" The pitch of her voice had risen in spite of her efforts to subdue it. "Ever since he was conceived, I've wanted him, known he was a special gift from God. How dare you belittle a miracle!''

"Wait a minute. I wasn't doing anything of the kind," Clay shot back. "Suppose something happened to you, or the kid needed something you couldn't afford? What then? Jess is a great little guy. Why should he have to go without amenities just because you're too proud or too stubborn to identify the SOB who got you pregnant?''

"Are you quite through?''

"I guess so.''

"Good," she said, breathing hard. "Then I'll thank you to get the hell out of my life and stay out.''

"What about Jess?''

"What about him?'' Sami was so angry she could hardly focus her thoughts.

"Paternity. You are going after the guy, aren't you? There's a detective I can recommend to do the legwork if you're not sure where Jess's father is these days. Name's Dick Rasmussen. He's very good.''

"Will you stop!''

"If money's a problem, Rasmussen can charge it to me. I don't mind.''

"Well, *I* do.'' Sami was gripping the receiver with both hands, her knuckles white, her whole body trembling. "Look, Clay, I'll try to explain this one more time. I will raise my son all by myself, the way I've always planned. I do *not* want you to go looking for his father, and I'll deny everything even if you do find some poor slob to pin it on, is that clear?''

"Perfectly.'' Teeth clenched, he kept himself from expressing his colorful opinion of her stubbornness. Waiting for her to bid him goodbye, he wasn't too surprised to hear the click of a broken connection instead of the usual parting pleasantries.

Cursing to himself, Clay made his way to the refrigerator, found a cold Coors and headed for the sanctuary of his den to pop the top on the beer and drink it. Settling himself in his favorite chair, he wondered how long it would be before Rasmussen located Vicki. So far, all the investigator had been able to ascertain was that she wasn't wanted by the police.

Clay took a series of slow swallows from the can. Considering the awful row he'd just had with Sami, her sister's innocence was damn poor consolation.

Chapter Six

By Friday, the good news was that the archaeologist hadn't found any bones of ancient Native Americans within the proposed perimeters of the Sycamore development.

The bad news was that Dick Rasmussen hadn't found Vicki, either. He'd concluded that she was either using another name or had moved out of the state.

Since the latter was unlikely, judging by Sami's previous comments, Clay supposed his ex was shacking up with some guy as usual and living off her boyfriend's credit cards rather than her own. That would be just like her. She was so capricious and irresponsible, she hadn't even changed the old address on her driver's license from when they'd been married!

Clay's forehead creased in a frown. Damn woman. You'd think she'd dropped out of sight for the express purpose of thwarting him. Dick was still working on locating her, but the way things were going, it looked as if any positive developments in the case would probably come too late to be of help.

Out of options, Clay headed for Sami's one last time. Given no choice, he'd see if she was still willing to contact Vicki on his behalf. If not, he might as well declare bankruptcy, salvage what he could and retire to Mexico, because he was finished on the West Coast.

Turning onto Cheney Street, he slowed. Up ahead, he could see Sami walking along the sidewalk, her legs long and tanned below the cuffs of her white shorts. Her midriff was bare, a white knit halter top showing off her figure to wondrous advantage. He'd never seen her dressed so revealingly, and the sight took his breath away.

"Wow," Clay muttered in appreciation, quickly regaining his composure. Sami was pushing Jess down the sidewalk in a blue-and-gray stroller. This was a stroke of authentic luck. Considering the way the rest of his week had gone, he figured if anyone deserved a dose of good fortune for a change, he certainly did.

Clay pulled up beside Sami and rolled down his window. "Hello there."

Instantly tense and uneasy, she glanced at him, then kept on walking.

"Nice day."

Sami ignored his overtures, but Jess scooted around and leaned out over the side of the stroller to study him as they all moved along.

"Hi, sport. What's up?" Clay asked, not really expecting an answer.

"Hi!" The little boy began to grin.

"How are you?"

"Okay."

Clay let his car creep alongside the curb to keep even with Sami's increasing pace. "Good. How's your mother?"

"I dunno." Jess twisted backward to look up at her over his shoulder, as if wondering why she didn't speak to the familiar man, too.

Reaching a corner, Sami paused at the crosswalk to wait for the traffic signal to turn green, then proceeded across the street and into the black asphalt parking lot of the Safeway Market.

Once there, she cut back and forth through the vacant spaces and ducked in the supermarket's sliding door before Clay could pull the car into an empty spot and park.

By the time he, too, entered the market, she'd left her stroller near the entrance and put Jess into the basket of a shopping cart. Grabbing a cart for himself so he wouldn't look too conspicuous, Clay pushed it down the main aisle, peering both ways at each side branch till he spotted his quarry.

Jess saw him coming and brightened instantly. "Hi!"

Barely glancing back, Sami turned a quick corner and sped away through the deli section. Clay cut left past the eggs and margarine, skidded along the front of the milk cooler and headed her off in fresh pasta. When he got to within ten or fifteen feet, he heard Jess laughing and saw him pointing and peeking out from behind his mother's body.

Once again, Sami took evasive action. By the time she finally reached the fruit-and-vegetable department, she'd toured the entire store at a run and was breathing pretty hard. Cornering her beside an enormous bin of watermelons, Clay put one foot on the rung at the bottom of his shopping cart and rode it the last few feet like a scooter. "Howdy. Fancy meeting you here."

She scowled at him.

"Want to play some more? I'll give you a head start."

"No, thanks."

That was better, he thought. She was speaking to him again. "Okay. Maybe later."

Jess giggled. "Yeah. Hi, Uncle Clay."

"Hi, kid. You got your safety belt on? Your mother's driving that thing like she thinks she's in the Indianapolis 500."

Looking down, Jess checked the narrow, red-webbing belt fastened tightly around his waist and nodded soberly.

"Good. Wouldn't want you to crash on those curves."

The little boy's big, dark eyes sparkled. "I like to race. It's fun. More, Mama?"

"Not now, honey." Sami turned her full attention to Clay. "Well? You went to a lot of trouble to catch up with me. What is it you want now?"

"You look very pretty today." He eyed her skimpy summer outfit.

Sami blushed. She *knew* she should have thrown a baggy shirt on over the top before leaving the house. "Hopefully, that isn't why you chased me."

"No. Unfortunately it isn't. My investigator has covered all the usual avenues and can't find your sister."

"What else is new?"

"Nothing much, except I'm running out of time. If your offer is still good, I'd be willing to let you take my bid to her."

"That's big of you."

He shrugged. "Yeah. I know. I'm a louse. Only I'm also in deep you-know-what here. How about it? If I prepare a written proposal, will you deliver it for me?"

She couldn't help but feel sorry for him. As adamant as he'd been in rejecting her suggestion before, it was clear he had to be desperate to reconsider using her as a go-between.

Besides, Sami admitted, he looked absolutely wonderful. The past week without him had been the loneliest in her entire life. Running into Clay on the street just now had given her such an emotional and physical jolt, she'd fled without thinking, simply because his presence was heightening her personal awareness so intensely.

Pausing to think, Sami studied him. A lock of his dark hair had fallen in a loose wave over his forehead, his eyes were brilliantly spellbinding, and the corners of his sensitive mouth were turned up in a faint smile. At times like these, even though he was dressed like a businessman, sans suit jacket due to the heat, he looked so much like the young boy she'd loved, it was hard to remember he was all grown-up.

Well, she'd *better* remember, Sami told herself. As a tempting, attractive, adult man, Clay Ellis was eminently more hazardous to her future peace and happiness than ever before.

Guilt regarding *Clay's* future happiness flooded her entire being. Keeping him out of Jess's life wasn't fair, yet what else could she do? Logically, it would be idiotic to allow him greater access to the boy. Morally? Well, that was another side of the question, wasn't it? She'd spent the latter part of her childhood without parents to love and care for her, and the memories of that kind of loneliness never totally went away.

Maybe that was why she felt she had to focus her affection on Jess so completely, Sami thought. Perhaps that was also why her heart kept insisting Clay had a right to get to know the boy a little better, even if he never learned he was his father.

"All right," she finally said, deciding to comply with his sensible request, salve her conscience a bit and also hasten his eventual departure. "Come to the house for dinner tonight and bring the papers. We'll discuss it then."

He breathed a sigh of genuine relief. "Thanks." Smiling at Jess, he asked, "Can I bring something tonight? Wine? Flowers? Animal crackers?"

Sami chuckled. "That won't be necessary. I'll take care of everything. Just come at seven and be ready to plead your case. If I think it sounds fair to my sister, I'll carry your message to her."

"Will it take long to make the round trip?"

She eyed him dubiously. "You never quit, do you? You must think I'm dumb as that rutabaga over there if you think I haven't figured out that the more I tell you, the easier it will be for you to skip using me altogether and find Vicki yourself."

"Can't blame a guy for trying."

"Yes, I can. And I do. See that you play it straight with me or the deal's off."

Raising one eyebrow, he saluted. "You got it. Anything else?"

"Yes. How about getting your cart out of my way and letting me do my shopping? I may work out of an office in my house, but that doesn't mean I have time to waste."

"Till tonight, then," he said, waving to Jess. The child returned the friendly gesture and Sami wondered if she was the only person in the world who noticed how much alike the two looked and acted, from their hair, eyes and smiles right down to the simplest mannerisms. She didn't see how anyone who had any powers of observation at all could miss the obvious biological connection.

"He's coming for dinner?" Eleanor asked, her expression betraying contagious enthusiasm.

"Yes." Sami was halfway through damp-mopping her kitchen floor, and her amiably nosy neighbor was leaning in the doorway, watching.

"You don't seem nearly as excited as I'd be."

"There's nothing to get excited about," Sami lied, feeling her pulse begin to hammer when she pictured Clay seated at her dining room table, eating with her and Jess.

The whole scenario of a happy, complete family was preposterous, of course. She knew that. So why did she keep picturing Clay as an integral part of her life? What a masochistic thing to do!

And why in heaven's name had she invited him to dinner when a simple business meeting would have sufficed? she wondered. Jess was already so captivated by the man it was scary. To encourage their interaction was sheer folly, yet in some obscure way she felt compelled to let them get better acquainted. It was as if her conscience and her heart had joined forces against her more logical side and won sovereignty, at least temporarily.

Finishing the floor, she wrung out the yellow sponge mop and returned it to the broom closet. Eleanor was still hanging around, a satisfied smile on her face.

"So, you're not at all dithered because the hunk is invited for dinner."

"That's right," Sami said.

"Then how come you just stuck your wet mop in the pantry?" Eleanor asked with a leer. "Don't tell me you've started keeping it there all the time."

"I didn't..." But Sami realized she had done exactly that. And if her friend hadn't mentioned the silly error, the mop would undoubtedly have remained there until she fell over it trying to get to the food.

Sami pulled a face. "Okay. So I may be just a little out of it today. I've had a rough week. The last two articles I wrote for the *Express* were hacked to pieces by my editor and the one before that was rejected altogether." She took a head of lettuce out of the crisper and began to wash it at the sink. "Sometimes I think I would have made a better ditchdigger."

"Or clerk in a donut shop. My father always said I'd be good at that, but I decided having kids was my gift. A lot of women hate staying home and being somebody's mommy, but I honestly love it."

"Me, too," Sami said, smiling. "I don't know what I'd do without Jess."

"Yeah, I know what you mean." Eleanor stepped up to the refrigerator and opened the door. "Got a diet cola I can mooch?"

"In the door. Hand me the box of cherry tomatoes, too, will you? I'm going to make the salad now so I don't have to fix it at the last minute."

Eleanor laughed as she set the tiny tomatoes on the sink and popped the top on the fizzy can. "Where are you going to put it when you get it finished—in the broom closet?"

"Very funny."

"*I* thought so." She rested one of her ample hips against the edge of the counter while she drank. "Anything I can do to help? Except wash the windows, I mean. I don't do windows."

"Not that I can think of," Sami said, "although, judging by my earlier performance with the mop, there's no telling how this meal will turn out. Maybe I should just order a pizza with all the trimmings and forget about cooking."

"Sounds good to me. Want me to watch Jess for you tonight so you and your date can have some time alone?"

Alone? Suddenly feeling wobbly, Sami grasped the edge of the sink to steady herself and hoped her companion hadn't noticed the telling reflex. "He's not my date," she insisted. "And I want Jess to be here. He and Clay seem to enjoy each other's company."

"Good plan," Eleanor said. "Get the guy involved with the kid early in the game instead of waiting till later when he might balk."

Sami shook her head adamantly. "It's nothing like that. This whole meeting tonight is strictly on account of my sister. Once Clay has gotten what he wants from Vicki, I'm sure he'll disappear as quickly as possible.''

"Unless *you're* what he really wants," Eleanor observed casually, taking a series of sips from the icy red, white and blue can.

Sami's heart lurched and her stomach came to rest with a thud somewhere close to her Adam's apple. "That's impossible. I've told him over and over that I have no romantic interest in him.''

The older woman laughed out loud. "Okay. Protest all you want. But you'd better wipe that spacey, dreamy look off your face and stop sighing all the time, if you mean to be convincing. So far, you haven't even come close to making me believe you, and Bennie says I'm easier to snow than anybody he's ever known.''

"It shows that badly?" Sami asked quietly, biting her lower lip.

"Yes.''

"Damn. I suppose I'm going to have to try harder, huh?''

"If you intend to fool him for long, you sure are. The thing is, why hide how you feel? Enjoy yourself, Sami. Don't waste all your love on one little boy when you could probably have a full life with a wonderful man just for the asking.''

"Loving Jess is *not* a waste," she snapped back, even though she recognized the buried truth in what Eleanor was trying to tell her. "And he is my whole life. End of story.''

"That's too bad," her friend said, tucking the now-empty soda can into a recycling bin under the sink and turning to leave. "Well, see ya.''

"Yeah. Maybe tomorrow.''

Pensive, Sami wondered if her present facial expression also betrayed just how much she agreed with Eleanor's casual observations. A *lot* of things were too bad, not the least of which were her prior broken relationship with Clay Ellis and the impossibility of rebuilding it.

By the time Clay arrived, bearing a fresh bouquet of daisies again in spite of her insistence he needn't bring her anything special, Sami had managed to put together a fairly impressive dinner.

The broiled chicken was well-done, the way he preferred it, the baked potatoes were crispy on the outside and cooked all the way through, and the green salad had managed to survive a few hours without refrigeration when she'd forgotten to put it away after completing it.

"Come on in," Sami said, hoping she succeeded in concealing her apprehensiveness at his arrival.

"Thanks." He handed her the bouquet. "These are for you."

Hearing Clay's deep voice, Jess came running, heading straight for him, his arms outstretched. Reaching down, Clay scooped him up with ease. "Hi, little buddy. You been good today?"

Jess nodded with vigor. "Uh-huh. I got a fire truck. Wanna see?"

"Sure." Clay succumbed to the boy's rapid squirming and set him down, smiling fondly as he watched him scamper off to locate the toy. "He's quite a kid," he said, turning his attention to Sami.

"Yes, he is."

"You look very pretty tonight."

"Thanks. So do you," she said, before realizing how silly the statement sounded. He'd rolled up the sleeves of his shirt, shed the tie and opened the collar. *Sexy* was a much more accurate description. Darn it.

Clay was grinning at her. "Is that a new dress?"

"No. I've had it for ages." The filmy, gauzelike, pink-and-purple tie-dyed dress had come from a charming little boutique in San Francisco. She and Vicki had been on one of many shopping expeditions, killing time till Jess was born. Purchasing the unusual garment had been nothing but a silly whim, one Sami wouldn't have given in to if it hadn't been for her sister's urging.

"Buy it!" Vicki had insisted with far more enthusiasm than Sami was feeling. "It's perfect for you."

"I don't know...." Twirling in front of the full-length mirror in the seaside shop, Sami had tugged on the ties at the front of the scooping neckline and felt as if she were looking at a stranger. "It's so... *thin*."

Vicki giggled. "It's supposed to be, silly. It's gauze. You wear lacy stuff under it unless you're alone with a special guy. Then you don't wear anything."

"Vicki!"

The younger woman made a disgusted face. "Oh, give me a break. You're such a stuffy prude. Buy the dress. If you don't want to keep it, you can give it to me when I'm back to normal." She patted her distended abdomen. "God, I hope that's soon."

Once Sami had gotten the lovely garment home and tried it on again, she'd decided immediately that the bodice was cut too low and the flowing, full skirt was far too long. Vicki had convinced her to keep it, but Sami still thought it made her look like a wandering gypsy. Intending to give the dress to her sister someday, this was the only time she'd worn it.

Clay was studying her. "I like those bright colors on you for a change. They seem to make your eyes look even bluer than usual." He smiled.

Sami wished she could come up with a witty retort, but her mind refused to cooperate. It did occur to her, however, that her traitorous subconscious must have had a hand in the selection of that particular dress for tonight's dinner.

The last thing she'd meant to do was appear more appealing to Clay, yet she'd put on the only dress in her closet that had been defined as *enticing* by an expert. Remembering Vicki's words, she flushed crimson. At least she was wearing nontransparent undergarments!

"Dinner is almost ready," Sami said, simultaneously recovering her voice and élan as her son returned to stand excitedly between them, holding up the red truck for everyone to admire. "Why don't you two boys go play with Jess's truck while I put the food on the table?" Cradling her bouquet in the crook of her arm, she started for the kitchen.

"I'll come help you."

Sami paused. "That won't be necessary." *Go play with your son,* she thought. *This is probably the last chance you're going to get.*

"Okay," Clay said, shrugging. "If that's what you want. Holler when you're ready for us."

As she watched him crouch down and begin to quietly admire the toy, Sami's throat tightened, her eyes filling with unshed tears. *Oh, God, look at them. They're perfect together. Man and boy, father and son.*

In self-defense, she turned away, stood straighter, lifted her chin in denial of the truth that was so evident, and took a deep, shuddering breath. Tonight was absolutely the last time she'd permit this kind of folly. Jess and Clay might truly like each other, even fulfill a mutual need, but she couldn't stand to see them together anymore. The rightness of it was far too painful.

Chapter Seven

As soon as Sami announced that dinner was ready, Clay marched Jess to the bathroom so they could wash up before eating. They were in there so long Sami began to wonder why.

Returning together, Jess and Clay both looked far too smug and self-satisfied to suit her. "All right," she said, hands on her hips. "What's going on?"

"We'll talk about it later," Clay said, giving Jess a wink. He held Sami's chair for her and she sat down, but he could tell she wasn't satisfied with his vague response.

Jess had clambered up onto the booster seat he always used, leaving two empty chairs across the table from Sami. Clay seated himself in the closest, unfolded his white linen napkin and laid it on his lap.

Frowning at the empty space beside his own place setting, Jess demanded a napkin, too.

"You'll just drop it on the floor like you always do," Sami told him. "I'll wipe your mouth if it needs it." She began dishing up his food, taking care to supply small enough portions and cutting up his chicken so that he wouldn't have too much trouble handling it all by himself.

Instead of eating, Jess began to pout, keeping at it till he managed to squeeze a few tears out of his tightly shut eyes.

"Here. You can have mine," Clay said, refolding his napkin and holding it out across the table to the little boy.

Sami intervened. All she had to do was raise an eyebrow and speak to Clay with the irate fire of her glance and he got the message.

"Sorry, kid," he said, withdrawing his offer. "Your mother's right. You take care of the eating part and she'll do the rest."

Her head cocking to one side, she nodded. "Thank you, *Mr.* Ellis."

"You're welcome, *Ms.* Adamson."

The sarcasm in both their voices and the looks on their faces seemed to amuse Jess, because he suddenly forgot all about being upset, switched his concentration to the two adults, and giggled instead.

Sami passed the platter of chicken to Clay. "I assume you brought along the papers you want me to take to my sister."

"Yes. They're in my briefcase, in the car. I thought, after dinner, maybe we could move out onto the porch, sit in the glider like we used to, and I could bring you up to speed on the particulars."

The glider. They'd met there often in the distant past. Like the night before Clay left for college. As usual, they'd gotten around to the subject of her unruly sister.

"You really think you can handle her all by yourself?" Clay had asked.

"Of course I can. She's just young and foolish. It's a temporary condition. Vicki's no dummy. She'll settle down pretty soon."

"And do what? Are you going to support her for the rest of her life?"

"Of course not. She's only fifteen. She has years yet to decide what career she wants to pursue."

"And in the meantime?" Clay had asked, reaching for her hand. "What about your life, your dreams, your career?"

"Vicki needs me. I'm all she has. There'll be plenty of time for me to go to college later. If we both worked, maybe we could make it through, together."

Clay had laughed then, angering her, and she had pulled from his tender grasp, but in retrospect he was right, of course. Vicki had never intended to continue her education, nor was she willing to help Sami do so. If it hadn't been for the night classes she'd taken in between bouts of rescuing her sister from one scrape after another, Sami wouldn't have been able to afford any higher education at all.

She and Clay had shared more than one deeply personal exchange while under the spell of the slow, peaceful rhythm of the porch glider, sometimes staying up half the night to talk, without realizing how much time had passed. The swing was a symbol of their youth. Their missed opportunities. A sense of risky déjà vu washed over her.

"I don't see any reason to waste time," Sami said. "Why don't we go ahead and discuss business while we eat?"

"I didn't think making polite conversation was a waste of time. We've had precious little chance to just kick back and get to know each other again."

"Why is that important?" Sami's hand trembled as she lifted the salad bowl, and she quickly set it down to hide her jitters.

"I thought maybe, when all this is over, we could forget about Vicki and concentrate on just the two...excuse me—three...of us."

"That isn't possible," Sami said, staring directly at him and hoping Eleanor was wrong about her transparently evident attraction to the man.

"Why not?" Clay put his fork down and scowled at her.

"It just isn't."

"Because you don't want anyone else in Jess's life? Is that it?"

"I never said that."

"You didn't have to. It's written all over your face. Somehow you've gotten the crazy idea that you can be a superwoman and adequately take the place of two parents all by yourself."

"It's not crazy. I'm doing it."

"Are you?" He glanced at the little boy who was busy chasing several loose green peas around the edge of his plate with a large fork. "It's not only crazy, it's selfish. I take it you're happy with the way he's developing?"

"Of course I am."

"Okay. It must have been really hard to potty-train him, considering."

"He makes a mistake once in a while, but that's to be expected." She made a face at Clay. "This isn't simple rhetoric, is it? Well, go ahead. Make your point."

Clay caught Jess's eye and smiled at him. "Want to tell her, buddy?"

Jess nodded enthusiastically. What followed was a two-year-old's vivid description of the differences in male and female anatomy and the definite advantages of being a boy when going to the bathroom. Sami had to fight hard to keep a straight face through it all, finally pressing her napkin to her lips to cover her grin and stifle the giggles.

"I see," she said as the dissertation concluded. "How interesting."

"Yeah," Jess said. "It was fun."

"I'd never thought of it quite like that," she said, straight-faced.

She almost broke up when her son cracked back, "Me neither."

One eyebrow raised, she peered over at Clay. "Was that really necessary?"

"I thought so. He was having a hell of a time doing it your way."

"I see." Blotting her lips, she gazed at her lap long enough to regain control of her sense of humor. "In that case, thank you."

"Glad to help."

Quietly cutting her chicken from the bone, she decided it was well past time to change the subject. As the parent of a young child, she was used to unusual dinner conversation, but enough was enough. "So. Tell me more about your project and why finding Vicki is so critical."

Clay picked up his fork and speared a bite, chewing and swallowing it before answering. "The Sycamore Plaza is the biggest mall I've ever tried to put together. It will give the city an enormous amount of revenue, and I've already worked out a deal to split the first year's sales taxes. Three major stores have agreed to participate—we call them the anchors—and I have nearly half the rest of the square footage rented."

"Sounds impressive."

"It will be," Clay said, taking a deep, slow breath. "But only if I can get Vicki to agree to part with the piece of land I gave her as a wedding present."

"*That* sounds tacky."

He nodded. "I know. Which is why I didn't try to get it from her during our divorce. The trouble is, my current financial partners decided to press ahead with this project without telling me until it was too late to call it off. People and money are committed. I'm into it for just about all I could beg, borrow or steal, too. If I don't succeed with your sister, I'll be ruined and take innocent investors down with me. I don't want to do that."

"Of course not!"

"Well, will you help me?"

Sami shot him a disgusted look. "All you'd have had to do was tell me this to begin with and I'd have done whatever I could for you."

"But then I'd have had to admit to financial problems."

"So?"

Clay smiled over at her. "You were always so proud of me. I didn't want that to change, Sami. Not even if it cost me everything."

"That's dumb," she grumbled.

Chuckling, he agreed. "I never claimed it wasn't."

Adding more butter to her baked potato, she thought for a moment and formulated a plan. "Okay. Be here bright and early tomorrow morning, say by nine, and I'll run the contracts or whatever over to Vicki. It's too late to go tonight." She failed to mention that Mac and the SinSeers were in concert that evening and her sister would be hanging around with the other groupies backstage instead of sitting at home, anyway.

"I'm not even going to ask how long you'll be gone," Clay said. "Are you planning on taking Jess with you? If not, I could watch him. After all, you will be doing me a big favor. I may as well return it."

Sami felt a softness, an unexpected tenderness toward Clay, come over her. He actually wanted to be with Jess. She could tell. And judging from the twinkle in her son's eyes as he looked at her expectantly, the boy felt the same. "Okay, but no more acrobatic bathroom lessons."

Grinning broadly, Clay nodded. "Agreed. Anything else?"

"Not that I can think of offhand. I'm sure you two will come up with lots of other ways to get in trouble, though."

He laughed and winked at the boy. "Probably."

Jess giggled in reply and echoed, "Pro'bly."

Sami felt like she was looking in a magic mirror and seeing two almost identical versions of the same imp. Both were so dear it hurt to look at them.

Jess was asleep on the couch, propped up in the corner like a rag doll, his head on the arm, his feet dangling toward the floor, when Clay picked him up and carried him to bed. He stood back as Sami got her little one into his summer pajamas and took him to the bathroom one last time.

The sweet picture of familial bliss burned itself into Clay's mind and heart. This was what life was supposed to be like. A man needed a safe sanctuary to retreat to when the outside world started to get to him, a place where somebody accepted him as he was and where he could be tender and playful without seeming powerless or weak.

But how could he ever explain that to Sami? He shook his head. He couldn't. At least, not yet. When and if the right time did come and he tried once again to reach through her defenses and touch her heart, he hoped she wouldn't think less of him for it. In the meantime, he had a company to rescue.

Tiptoeing out into the hall, Sami rejoined Clay. "He fell right to sleep."

"Good." Clay put his arm lightly around her shoulders and walked her down the stairs. "Do you want me to go out and get the contracts now?"

"I suppose you might as well." If she could have stopped time and stayed with him just as they were, their little boy happily asleep upstairs, the house calm, the mood tranquil, she would have. In a heartbeat. But, of course, such daydreams were nothing more than a cruel illusion.

He led her to the front door. "Come on. The glider's waiting."

"No. It's too dark and cold out there," she alibied.

"We'll turn on the porch light." He wanted to tell her he'd be glad to keep her warm against the night chill, but figured he was better off concentrating on the lack of illumination instead. Consciously he removed his arm from around her shoulders.

"The bulb is burned-out."

"Then I'll replace it for you while I'm here."

"Clay, I..." Sami was hanging back, her breathing growing ragged, her heart racing.

"I know," he said, trying not to show the full extent of his disappointment. "You don't want to be alone with me."

"I didn't say that."

"You didn't have to."

Contrite, she was first through the door. "Okay. You win. We're as much alone *in* the house as out of it, I guess. Go get your briefcase. I'll dust off the stupid swing."

Smiling to himself, he jogged down off the porch, got what he needed and hurried back to find her already sitting on the wooden swing and pushing it back and forth lazily with her feet.

"You didn't need to run," she said.

"I wasn't taking any chances you might change your mind and lock me out."

Sami grimaced. "You mean like before? I'm sorry about that. I guess I was pretty overtired that day. Everything had gone wrong and, well, I just fell apart."

"Have you been happy the last few years?" he asked, placing the brown leather case between them on the seat and joining her.

"Of course I have."

"I suppose that's a judgment call, anyway," Clay said, nodding. "Some people are happy no matter what, and others never are. I guess I fall somewhere in the middle."

"Your business is good. You should be thankful for that."

"I am." Opening the case, he withdrew a beige envelope containing the papers he needed his ex-wife to sign. "Speaking of which, here's all you'll need. I also brought along a copy of the architect's rendering of the exterior of Sycamore Plaza, if you'd like to see it."

"Sure." She looked at the drawing, and the scope of the project amazed her. "Wow!"

"Yeah. It's impressive. If I ever get it built, that is."

"You will." She smiled at him. "I've never doubted your capabilities."

Clay reached over and took her hand, placing it between both of his and caressing it. Then he raised it to his lips.

Getting to her feet, she tried to pull away.

He, too, arose and held her fast. "Don't do this to us, Sami. I don't know if we can ever recapture what we almost had once, but I'm willing to try."

"Well, I'm not."

"Why not? Because I made a stupid mistake and married the wrong sister? Is that it?" He cursed. "I swear, if there was any way to undo that mistake, I would. All I can do is promise to spend every moment of the rest of my life making it up to you."

"No!" She tugged at her hand to free it, with little success. It was the look of fear and revulsion in her expression that made him voluntarily release her.

"Vicki cheated on me over and over," he said in his own defense. "What was I supposed to do—continue to forgive her forever? Damn it, Sami, I tried to save the marriage. Don't blame me because your sister is a tramp."

"Stop talking about her like that." She was rubbing her hands together, trying to make the unexplainable chill she was suddenly sensing go away.

"Why? It's true. Maybe if you faced facts for a change, you wouldn't be so quick to condemn me."

"I never accused you of doing anything wrong. You just assumed I did because you figured you knew all about everything, as usual. Well, you were wrong." She headed for the door, ready to defend her sister more, if necessary. It wasn't.

Clay, already on his feet, picked up the papers Sami had dropped in her haste to get away from him, returned them to the envelope and laid it on the seat of the glider.

"I'll be here at 9:00 a.m. sharp," he said. "And don't worry. I won't bother you again after that. Once we've concluded our business, I'll do what you obviously want me to do and get the hell out of your life for good."

Nodding, her eyes downcast, she clenched her fingers together in front of her till they hurt. "That's best. Trust me. I know I'm right."

"Right or wrong, I can't very well carry on a love affair with you if you won't participate."

The word, *love,* shot straight to Sami's heart and echoed there, refusing to be silenced. She closed her eyes. When she opened them again because she sensed his nearness, smelled his after-shave, felt the warmth of his body, Clay was standing directly in front of her.

He took two fingers, placed them gently beneath her chin and lifted, tenderly guiding her mouth to meet his.

Sami's lips parted in a gasp. Before that instant, she'd felt trapped by Clay's superior strength, and the perception, however undeserved, had caused her to resist, to want to flee. Suddenly, without warning, all that had changed and the absence of her usual ingrained reticence was hard to deal with.

Clearly confused by the conflicting emotions Clay was arousing within her, Sami felt like she was floating in a cloud of sensation. This kiss was different from any she had received before. So was her instinctive reaction to it.

Sliding her hands up his chest, she slipped her arms around his neck, stood on tiptoe and returned the simple affection he offered. She didn't want to hurt Clay. She never had. And she didn't see any reason to prolong the pain of parting for either of them, it was just that this particular kiss seemed so right, so perfect a joining, she was loath to let him go.

Hearing him groan, feeling him pulling away from her, she wasn't sure what she'd done wrong.

He grasped her wrists and forcibly lowered her arms, holding them there. "No more, Sami. I'm not made of stone, you know."

"Neither am I," she said without thinking.

Clay's glance swept over her body, leaving her with a sense of nakedness that had little to do with the thin fabric of her dress. "No, you certainly aren't."

His voice was raspy, sort of breathless, and the enigmatic timbre of it made her skin tingle. She shivered. "I told you it was chilly tonight."

"No," Clay said with a cynical chuckle. "Tonight it's way too hot for me. I'd better be going."

Sami didn't want him to leave, yet she didn't dare ask him to stay, for fear he might. The special moment they had just experienced had shaken her to the core. She knew she couldn't have been instantly cured of her ingrained aversion to having sex. That was impossible. However, *something* odd had certainly happened a few moments ago. Whatever it was, it was evident Clay had also been affected.

"Good night, then," Sami said softly, the gentle regard in her tone rippling along her skin and making her doubly aware of the mutual bewitchment of their spirits. "Have a safe trip home."

"Don't worry about that. I've decided to get a motel room in town. There's no sense driving all the way up to Victorville when I have to be back here early tomorrow."

"Circumstances being what they are, I don't think it would be a good idea to offer to let you stay the night with us," she said, her voice a near whisper.

Shaking his head, Clay agreed. "Neither do I. Good night, Sami."

Hugging herself against the chill, she watched him pick up his briefcase, walk briskly to his car, get in and drive away.

It was right to let him go. She knew that. So why was it so hard to keep from calling out to him and begging him to come back?

Slowly, pensively, Sami went to retrieve the manila envelope Clay had left for her, then entered the house, pulling the heavy front door closed and locking it behind her for the night.

The dinner dishes had been cleared from the dining room table, leaving only the bare linen tablecloth and the half-circle of crumbs and squashed green peas that denoted Jess's place.

She smiled to herself. Sweet little guy. Jess had tried so hard to impress Clay and he'd still made his usual mess.

Glancing up at the ceiling and picturing her son asleep in his bed in the room above, she sent a silent prayer of thanks heavenward.

A few moments later, she realized with a start that Clay Ellis had been as much a part of her thoughts of abject gratitude as Jess had. She sighed. There was sure more to this father-and-son thing than she'd first imagined, wasn't there?

Chapter Eight

Trying to concentrate solely on business matters, for her own sake as much as anything, Sami bustled around her office the following morning while waiting for Clay's arrival. She'd completed her current assignments with only hours to spare and sent them via modem to the newspaper office.

Since then, she hadn't heard a word from the features editor, so she figured her work was acceptable. At least, she hoped so. Lately, with all she'd had on her mind, there was no guarantee.

Determined to make Vicki feel as relaxed as possible, she'd decided to don an old pair of jeans and a black jeweled T-shirt her sister had given her that had unevenly spaced holes cut in the fabric. It was *not* something Sami would have worn under normal circumstances, and she'd spent several extra minutes in front of her dresser mirror making sure she was still decent in spite of the holes.

Dangling, shimmering, shoulder-duster earrings and sandals completed the outfit. Coming downstairs to answer

Clay's knock, it occurred to her that she could use the same outfit to dress up for Halloween and take Jess trick-or-treating.

The astonished look on Clay's face confirmed her conclusion. He shook his head. "For a wild second I thought you were Vicki."

Sami pirouetted for him. "It's sort of a costume. Vicki gave me most of this stuff, and I thought she'd feel more at ease if I wore it when I went to talk to her."

"That's smart," Clay said. "Did you get a chance to read all the information I left with you?"

"Yes. The deal seems quite reasonable to me. Hopefully, my sister will feel the same."

Sami stepped back and gestured for him to come in. So far, she was still able to confine the bulk of her thoughts to the project at hand. Good. As long as that continued, she might even be able to escape to her sister's before Clay's overpowering presence turned her brain into yesterday's oatmeal again.

"Jess has had breakfast and is playing in the backyard," Sami said, bustling about to avoid making eye contact with Clay. "You shouldn't have any trouble with him, but if you do, there are emergency and doctors' numbers here on a pad by the phone."

It struck him as cute, the way she was giving detailed instructions to him the same way she would to an immature teenager who happened to be baby-sitting. "Trust me, Sami. We'll be fine."

"I'm sure you will. There's tuna salad in the refrigerator for sandwiches—Jess likes white bread—and be sure you don't put pickles on his or he'll pitch a fit."

"No problem," Clay said. "I understand. You know I hate all forms of cucumbers, too, even when they're disguised."

Sami shot him a brief, unreadable glance. He supposed he should be thankful she was taking his business dealings so seriously, but he wished she were acting at least a little glad to see him. From her strange reaction, his dislike of cucumbers seemed like some kind of dreadful omen or something.

She slung the leather strap of her purse over her shoulder and patted the outside of the bag. "I have the envelope with the contract. Wish me luck."

Stepping forward, Clay was not at all surprised when she extended her right hand formally. He shook it as if she were no one special and quickly let go because that was how he sensed she wanted him to behave.

"Did you tell Jess I was coming today?"

"Yes. He seemed excited about the chance to have you all to himself. Said something about playing robots."

"He's great. Why don't you walk me out back so I don't startle him and get off on the wrong foot?"

"Good idea." Sami led the way through the kitchen, her back stiff, her demeanor that of a person totally focused on completing a difficult task and anxious to be on her way.

She opened the door and called to Jess, watched man and boy greet each other, then retreated back inside, alone. Her mouth was dry, her hands clammy, her nerves frayed.

Stopping at the sink for a glass of water, she made the mistake of glancing out the window at father and son. Clay had squatted down to the boy's level and was earnestly listening to every word Jess said. Animated and waving his tiny hands in the air, the toddler was obviously taking complete advantage of his rapt audience. Never before had Sami seen such a precious sight.

The resulting catch in her throat was nothing compared to the gigantic lump of unadulterated remorse sitting in the midst of her heart and the cascades of tears swelling up in her eyes.

The forgotten water glass shattered in the porcelain sink as Sami ran from the room and from the impossible vision of paradise she couldn't bear to look at for one more second.

Diamond Bar was an exclusive, horsey community located halfway between Riverside and the San Gabriel Valley. The McCall house, a low, sprawling ranch-style, stood at the end of a cul-de-sac behind tall, wrought-iron gates and a natural-colored, masonry stone wall. Closed-circuit television cameras guarded the perimeters both from burglars and from Mac's adoring fans.

Sami stopped her older car at the gate, climbed out and pressed the communications buzzer for admittance.

It was Vicki herself who answered. "Who is it?"

"It's me. Sami." She stepped back, arms held out in a show of innocence, so the camera could capture her entire facade.

"I got your messages. I've just been too busy to return your calls. You know how it is."

"Sure." Sami smiled into the camera lens. "Can we talk? I have some really good news for you."

"Now? Mac played a concert last night and I was up partying till after three in the morning. Can't it wait?"

"I'm afraid not." She heard what she thought was a sigh.

"Are you alone?"

"Totally."

"No kid?"

"He's at home." Sami was going to add details about who was baby-sitting, but decided that kind of trivial news would keep till she got inside.

"Okay."

A buzzer sounded and the heavy iron gate began to roll open on its track. Sami jumped back into her car and drove through. Following the circular drive, she admired the immaculate lawns and shrubs bordered by blooming petunias, miniature varieties of marigolds and several other colorful ground covers she couldn't identify. Obviously, Mac had one heck of a gardener.

Vicki answered the door clad in a floor-length black satin robe and matching slippers. She eyed her older sister's trendy clothing with cynical skepticism. "You came to join the band?"

"Not unless Mac needs a tambourine player. That's all I can handle." Sami started to reach for Vicki to hug her and was disappointed when she stepped away.

"Come on in. I need a drink. You want something?"

The hem of Vicki's robe swished against the polished terra-cotta tile floor as she led the way into a spacious den furnished entirely in modern black, white and chrome. Framed portraits of the SinSeers and two gold records graced the walls over the biggest, most lavish entertainment center Sami had ever seen.

"How about coffee?" Sami asked.

"Only if you make it. My head hurts too much and the cook has today off." Vicki pointed. "The kitchen's that way, through the arch."

"Never mind. I came to see you, not to drink coffee, anyway."

Vicki lifted a half-full tumbler of icy golden bourbon. "Cheers. Truthfully, I'm surprised to see you. The last time you were here, I seem to recall we didn't get along very well."

"Probably because I brought Jess along."

"Probably. No offense, but he reminds me of times and people I'd rather forget." She sipped her drink, pushed her thick, blond hair back off her forehead with inch-long crimson fingernails and sank onto the ebony leather couch, curling her feet under her. "So, what brings you here again? You sounded fairly frantic on the phone."

"Sorry if I worried you." Sami seated herself on the other end of the sofa and withdrew Clay's offer from her bag. "Your ex-husband asked me to bring this to you."

"He couldn't face me himself?"

"That's not it at all," Sami said in Clay's defense. "I wouldn't tell him where you were living, so he asked me to act as his liaison. He's about to make you rich."

Vicki laughed harshly. "Look around you. I'm already rich."

"Wrong," Sami said as delicately as she could. "Your boyfriend is the one with all the money. What happens when he finds someone else and gives you the boot?"

"He won't. Mac loves me." She squinted at the papers Sami was thrusting toward her. "You read them for me. I'm a little hung over this morning."

"Okay. But first I want you to know I've listened to Clay explain this project and I believe he's being fair with you."

Vicki shook her head. "I don't know what the hell you're talking about. What could I have that he wants?"

Starting at the beginning and remaining very business-like, Sami went over the details of the development, as well as Clay's generous offer. When she was through, Vicki got herself another drink and returned to the couch.

"Okay. What's the catch?"

"There isn't any," Sami swore. "He just got himself in a bind and couldn't locate you. I checked with two local real-estate companies to be sure the appraisal was fair, and it is. More than fair."

"So you're telling me I should sign?"

"Yes. You don't want the Sycamore property. You didn't even remember you owned it."

"That's true."

"And you could put the money in the bank where it will draw interest till you need it."

"Assuming I ever do."

Sami refused to allow herself to be jealous of her sister's extravagant life-style. In spite of Vicki's protestations of happiness, Sami knew better. There was no spark, no innate joy in her sister's face. As a matter of fact, someone not knowing which was the younger sibling might make a mistake. Years of hard living had taken their toll on Vicki's youthful beauty.

Offering the contract and a pen, Sami leaned back and waited. She'd said all she could on Clay's behalf. The deal *was* fair. Vicki would be a fool to turn it down.

"Okay. Where do I sign?" She set her drink down amid a cluster of overlapping, dried moisture rings on the glass coffee table.

"Right here. And tell me how you want the money. Shall I have him deposit it in an interest-bearing account?"

"Hell, you can bring it to me in a paper sack if you want. I don't care." She scribbled what passed for her name. "God, my head hurts."

"I am sorry. I'm really glad you didn't drink while you were pregnant, though. That can cause permanent damage to the baby." She gathered up her things and stood to leave.

"All right, all right. I know you expect me to ask. How is your precious little darling?"

Sami chose to ignore the sarcastic tone and simply answer the question. "Jess is fine. Growing like a weed. And so handsome. He's absolutely adorable." Just like his daddy, she added to herself.

"I'm surprised you trusted him with anyone else enough to let him out of your sight," Vicki said, accompanying her to the door. "You're actually worse about hovering over that kid than you were with me when I was little." She smiled slightly. "You drove me nuts."

"I know," Sami said. "I figured that was my job, with Mom and Dad gone." She paused to give her sister a brief hug on the way past. "Don't worry about Jess. He's with Clay."

Sami had reached her car before she heard Vicki say, "He's with *who?*"

"Clay," she called back.

"My Clay? Clay Ellis?"

"Uh-huh. He's real good with him."

Waving goodbye to her sister, while allowing her thoughts to focus on Clay and Jess, Sami sensed a familiar warmth and affinity flowing through her. As she drove away, she glanced in her rearview mirror and saw Vicki standing on the edge of the driveway, the full skirt of her black robe rippling slightly in the breeze, her hands on her hips.

If only she and her sister could somehow become friends, Sami thought. Absently, she doubted such an unlikely miracle would ever happen, but her optimistic nature insisted *anything* was possible. She'd certainly be receptive to Vicki's friendship if it was ever offered.

Clay was seated on the glider, Jess asleep in his lap, when Sami got home.

"How did it go?" he asked, afraid she'd had no luck, yet praying she'd succeeded.

"Fine." Sami waved the envelope containing the signed contract in triumph.

Clay's grin nearly split his face. "I'd jump up and down but it would wake my buddy here." He stroked the hair off Jess's forehead with his forefinger. "Poor little guy. He sweats when he first goes to sleep, just like I do."

"He should be in bed, anyway," Sami said, quickly turning away to avoid having to behold any more paternal tenderness. "It's almost time for his nap."

"We ate lunch like you said. No pickles." Clay lifted Jess, trying not to awaken him, and started for the door. "There's some tuna left if you're hungry. Tonight we'll get a real baby-sitter and I'll take you someplace fancy to celebrate."

She was staring off into the distance. "That won't be necessary. You don't have to reward me. I was glad to be able to do my sister a favor."

He'd have to have been deaf and blind to have missed Sami's allusion that she hadn't acted for his sake. "Go make yourself a sandwich," he said flatly. "I'll be right back."

Clay put Jess to bed, fully clothed except for his socks and tennis shoes, and hurriedly returned to Sami. She was in the kitchen, but so far had apparently made no effort to eat.

"He's still snoring away," Clay said in answer to her questioning look. "Now, what's this nonsense about not letting me treat you to a nice dinner?"

She handed him the folder containing the papers her sister had signed. The sooner she got him out of her house and out of her life, the sooner she could stop pretending she didn't care for him. It was getting harder and harder to maintain a disinterested appearance in spite of the lingering numbness in her heart. "I did what you asked. The way I see it, our business is concluded."

"Just like that?"

"Just like that, Clay. I'm glad I could help."

He snorted derisively. "Right. And now you want me to get lost, is that it?"

"Putting it that way is pretty crude, but yes."

"I take it you and Vicki got along fine?"

"As well as usual. You should be satisfied. It was good enough to get her to sign your contract."

"Were you able to answer all her questions about the project?" He'd gone to the refrigerator as they talked, gotten the plastic container of tuna salad and started to make Sami a sandwich as casually as if he lived there.

"She didn't ask any," Sami said. "I don't think she even cared."

"That's typical. How is she?"

Sami sighed. "Wasted." She shook her head slowly, sadly. "I wish I knew where I went wrong."

"Where *you* went wrong?" Clay put the sandwich on a plate, laid a dill spear beside it and brought it to her. "Don't be silly. You didn't do anything wrong."

Sami was too exhausted to reject the lunch he'd made for her, and besides, now that she'd seen and smelled the appetizing food, she realized how hungry she was. She took a seat at the kitchen table. "You seem awfully sure I was blameless."

He poured two tall glasses of iced tea and joined her. "I am sure. Remember, I knew both of you when we were kids. Vicki was always a lot like she is now. I don't think people change all that much from what they were to begin with."

"Maybe not." She took a bite. "Thanks for making this. I was hungrier than I thought."

"You're welcome. I have lots of good traits. I'd be happy to demonstrate, if you'd let me hang around here awhile longer." He paused, smiling slightly. "Hell, the *kid* likes me."

"I know he does. It's been good for him to get to know you, Clay. I just don't think it's wise to let him get too attached."

"I'm plenty attached myself," he said honestly. "After the past few weeks, it's hard to imagine not having you and Jess in my life all the time."

Sami put down the half-eaten sandwich and pushed herself away from the table. "Please don't, Clay. You'll just make it harder for me."

He captured her hand, but held it loosely. "I want it to be hard for you, Sami. So hard you can't send me away. So hard Jess looks for me around every corner. I'm not trying to torture you, honey, I'm trying to bring you into my life where you belong."

"No, Clay. No, no, no."

"One good reason. Give me one good reason and I'll go away."

The sharp voice that sounded from the doorway behind them was strident and its presence so totally unexpected it made them both start and jump apart.

"I'll give you a *damned* good reason," Vicki said, her eyes narrowing, focusing coldly on the couple she'd so brazenly interrupted. The tight black leather jumpsuit and gold chains she was wearing added to her threatening image and her high-heeled boots made her appear more imposing than usual.

Sami wheeled to face her sister. This couldn't be happening! Nightmares weren't this concrete.

"Well?" Vicki asked, concentrating more on Clay for the moment. "Aren't you interested?"

"Don't!" Sami begged. "Please!"

Staring, Vicki sneered. "Why not? I can see that lying runs in our family. Maybe telling the truth does, too. Do you suppose?"

Tears filled Sami's eyes. "Please, Vicki. For God's sake, don't." This was the ominous dream she'd had over and over, only now it felt far too real to be a mere by-product of her subconscious.

Concerned for Sami, Clay stepped forward, placed himself between the women and stood firm, glaring at his ex-wife. "What's going on, Vicki? First I can't find you anywhere and next you show up in your sister's house making vague threats and scaring her to death. Why? What can you hope to gain?"

"Maybe you should ask her."

The line of black kohl around Vicki's eyes had obviously been hurriedly applied, because it was more overdone than usual, Clay noted. Sami was right about her physical condition, too. She looked as if she'd been living a pretty hard life lately. Perhaps drug or alcohol abuse had finally unbalanced her mind.

"Leave Sami out of this," Clay said. "If you're upset about the deal we just made on the property, let's sit down and talk about it."

Vicki cursed. "You bet I'm upset. My sister is shacking up with a guy and talks me into practically giving him a valuable piece of land. Damn right, I'm upset."

Seeing how distressed Sami was, Clay put a steadying arm around her shoulders and gave her a squeeze of encouragement while he addressed the other woman. "Look, Vicki. I don't care how mad you get at me. I'm used to it. Only stop making idiotic accusations about Sami."

"Idiotic? Ha!"

"Knock it off, okay? You and I both know your sister is one of the most honest, upright people in the world. Unlike you, she doesn't tell lies. I know honesty is a foreign concept to you, but try to grasp it, will you?"

Angry beyond words, Vicki whirled away, sputtering epithets.

Trembling, but regaining control of herself, Sami stepped out of his protective grasp and spoke up. "Leave us alone, Clay. I'll handle this." When he didn't make a move to go, she added, "Please?"

"You're sure?" Out of the corner of his eye, he saw Vicki straightening the skintight, low-cut jumpsuit and smoothing it down over her hips. How two sisters could grow up with such obviously disparate morals he didn't know.

"If you leave, you'll miss all the fun," Vicki warned. "Don't you want to hear how your perfectly honest lover here put the lie of the century over on you?"

Clay stood firm. "I know better than to believe anything you tell me, Vicki, so don't bother trying to cause trouble between Sami and me. Your days of being able to do that were over long ago."

"Oh, really?" A twisted smile curled the corners of the younger woman's vividly painted mouth. "Then maybe you should just ask her who the brat's father is."

In Sami's tortured mind, that bold statement left her no more civilized options. Either she got Vicki and Clay apart while she reasoned with her sister to keep silent, or all her efforts to protect Jess—all her painful, difficult compromises of ethics—would be for nothing.

Launching herself in a flurry of fright and rage, Sami grabbed Vicki's arms and tried to force her back through the doorway into the hall. "Come on. We'll go outside and talk this out."

"No way!" Still surprisingly strong in spite of her dissipation, Vicki braced herself and leaned into the assault, screeching filthy words Clay hadn't heard since he'd worked on a construction crew.

"It doesn't matter," he shouted, trying to pull the two enraged women apart and restore peace. "I don't care *who* he was. Not anymore."

Vicki was hanging on to the doorjamb and kicking murderously to keep herself in place while she screamed, "Oh, no? Then ask her who the *mother* is!"

Chapter Nine

Dead silence ensued. Eyes wide and staring blankly, Sami sank back against the edge of the kitchen table. The charade was over, as surely as if Vicki had taken out a full-page ad in the *Express*.

Clay looked from one woman to the other, finally settling his full attention on Sami. "What is she talking about?"

Shoulders sagging, spirit broken, Sami merely shook her head and lowered her gaze to keep from having to see the disappointment that was certain to cross his face as soon as Vicki finished destroying her image.

"Well?"

"Leave me alone, Clay," Sami said, her voice nearly emotionless.

He took her hand. "No. Tell me what's wrong. You and I can work this out no matter what the circumstances of Jess's birth were. Don't you see that? I love you, Sami."

Vicki laughed cynically. "Oh, yeah? Well, how would it grab you if I told you that *I* was the kid's mommy?"

"Don't be ridiculous." He turned to Sami. "Tell me the whole story so your sister doesn't distort the facts, and then we'll put it all behind us."

This time, it was Sami who managed a wry chuckle. "I don't think we can, Clay." She hung her head. "No. I really don't think so."

Frustrated, he dropped her hand and paced across the kitchen. "Okay. Enough games. Somebody is going to tell me what the hell is going on here, because I'm not leaving till I get to the bottom of this."

Sami straightened. She'd been the one to actually mislead him; she should be the one to finally give him an unabridged version of the whole sordid mess.

"I might as well do it," she said, gathering her courage and lifting her head with determination. "At least that way you'll hear it without embellishments."

"Oh, thanks a heap," Vicki chimed in. "And I suppose pulling a fast one on your health insurance company was my idea, too?"

"I paid the doctor and hospital bills myself," Sami said. "It took me till last year, but I did it." She shot her sister a steely glance. "I only told you the pregnancy was covered by insurance so you wouldn't worry about how much money it was costing."

Vicki looked to Clay. "See? Another lie."

He leaned back against the edge of the kitchen counter and folded his arms across his chest. "Let Sami tell it," he said flatly. "I want to hear it from her."

"I was living in San Francisco," she began, her hands clasped tightly in front of her. "One day, Vicki showed up at my apartment and told me she was pregnant." Sami paused while Clay focused his scowl on the younger woman, then she resumed her story when he looked back at her.

"She wanted to get an abortion, but I talked her out of it. The deal was, she'd go ahead and carry the baby to term and then I'd take it and raise it as my own."

Clay nodded. "Okay. I can buy you doing that. But why lead me to believe you'd fallen for another man and Jess was the result? If you'd told me the truth in the first place, it wouldn't have changed the way I felt about him. He's just a little boy. He can't help who his real mother is."

"Thanks a lot," Vicki said.

He ignored her. Sami still looked too distraught to be through talking. "Go ahead. I get the feeling there's more."

She nodded. "There is." One quick glance at her sister and she knew there was no stopping now. The trouble was, she could hardly force herself to voice the details of the wrongdoing she'd kept hidden in her heart for so long.

"Vicki...I mean, we...decided the best way to avoid hassles about adoption, since I was single, was for us to switch identities whenever her pregnancy was involved. I never pretended to be the baby's natural mother. Vicki just used my identification for the doctor and the hospital."

"So that's how the records were handled," he said.

"Falsified," Vicki insisted. "The word is *falsified*."

Clay stared her down. "Go on, Sami. Finish it."

"There's not a whole lot more to tell. I took her to the hospital and coached her through the delivery and I fell in love with Jess the moment I saw him."

Vicki cocked her head. "That's not *quite* all."

The following few seconds would destroy her serenity— her *life*—as surely as if someone had exploded a bomb beneath her feet. Sami knew it. Yet Vicki was leaving her no choice. It was either confess to Clay herself or listen to her sister's version of what had transpired.

She took a deep breath and started. "What she means is, the timing was terrible for her. If you figure back, you'll realize your divorce wasn't final then. The reason she didn't want you to find out she was pregnant is because she didn't want anything to interfere with her getting a decree.'' She glared at her sister. ''Isn't that right?''

''Right as rain. But you're leaving out the best part. You never did know how to tell an entertaining story.''

Clay was holding up his hands, palms toward them, and staring from one sister to the other. ''Hold it. Somebody better spell it out for me before I lose my temper. What does all this have to do with Sami's lying to me? So far, I haven't heard anything that would make me think less of her. Maybe her methods weren't the ones I'd have chosen, but she did what she felt she had to do to save a baby's life and give it a good home. What's the big problem with that?''

Sami stood erect, squared her shoulders and took a tentative step toward him. ''I didn't want to lose my baby,'' she said, her voice coming out more steady than she felt.

He met her halfway. ''Of course, you didn't. I'll get my lawyers to look into the possible ramifications of your mistakes and we'll see what we can do to rectify them legally. It'll be all right.''

Letting him take her hands in his, she shook her head, tears welling in her eyes. This was it. The moment she'd forever remember as the instant when her well-ordered universe collapsed.

''You don't understand, Clay,'' Sami said. ''We think you're Jess's father.''

Vicki was applauding. ''Bravo! She finally spit out the whole truth. I thought she'd never get around to the juicy part.''

Leaving Sami, Clay approached his ex-wife and took her by the shoulders. ''You're lying. We weren't sleeping together then.''

''On the contrary. We might not have been living in the same house, but if you'll recall, we did have a real swinging goodbye party...just the two of us.''

He cursed. "That's impossible. You were on the Pill." The moment he looked into her eyes, he knew that for once she was being honest with him.

"Nope." She shrugged and smiled. "I lied."

In shock, and angry beyond words, Clay glared at the sisters, hardly able to swallow what he'd just learned. The contrite look of abject suffering on Sami's face, in her misty eyes, confirmed his worst fears. Whether he liked it or not, whether it was true or not, he was going to have to accept the fact that Sami believed it. That meant she'd deliberately deceived him. Knowing she'd played him for an idiot was what hurt the most. He couldn't stand there and watch her one more second.

Clay gritted his teeth, whirled and stormed out the door, heading for his car and the solitude the open highway offered. He had to get away from there and think. Good God, if what Vicki had surmised was true, he had a *son*.

Seconds later, he realized what was at the heart of his disappointment and indignation. Sami hadn't been lying simply to protect the boy from the law, she'd expressly intended to keep him from ever finding Vicki and possibly learning that Jess was his.

But was he? Could he believe everything a woman like that claimed? Yes, there had been a goodbye celebration of sorts. Vicki had showed up at his house one evening with a magnum of champagne in one hand and her lawyer's idea of an amicable settlement in the other.

As eager to be free as she was, he'd agreed to one toast, then another, till the rest of the evening became mostly a blur. He supposed, as crazy as Vicki was, she could have planned the whole lusty night, intending to use it against him in divorce court, if necessary, then had her plans backfire on her when she discovered she was pregnant as a result.

One thing was certain, he decided with total commitment, he was going to get his lawyers involved as soon as possible. If Jess was truly his son, he'd be damned if he'd let a couple of deceitful, conniving, dishonest sisters rob him of the pleasure of being a part of the boy's life.

Clay felt his gut spasm. He'd loved Sami. Trusted her. Grown to love her little boy, too. How could she have acted so perfectly innocent and natural while hiding such a cruel secret? Did she really think he was so self-centered he'd have taken the boy away from her? Snorting derisively, he picked up the cellular phone in his car and called his office.

"Judith," he said as soon as his secretary answered. "I have the signed deed to my ex-wife's property, but there may be a catch. She's pitching a fit and claiming collusion. Chances are very good we may be sued."

"You do have a way with women," she gibed. "What's our next move?"

"Get me an appointment with my lawyers—George, if he's available. Make it for next week sometime. And call Rasmussen for me."

"Again?"

"Again. I thought we were done with our investigation, but it looks like I was wrong."

"Are you okay?" she asked with concern.

"I'm not sure." Clay shook his head slightly. "My life is beginning to sound like a live soap opera."

"Maybe you can sell the rights to the story and make a fortune?"

He chuckled. Talking to Judith always helped improve his disposition, no matter how gloomy it had been to begin with. "Nobody would believe it," he said. "Even I have trouble sometimes."

"Well, don't worry too much. These things have a way of working out for the best, given enough time."

"Spoken like a typical woman," he said, chiding her. "Personally, I feel like hitting someone or something till I can't lift my arm to pound on it anymore."

"But you won't."

"No, I suppose not. No matter how mad I get, I probably won't act out my aggressions."

"Which separates us from cavemen."

"Unfortunately."

Clay pictured himself, naked except for a bearskin loincloth, carrying a hefty club and dragging Sami back to his cave while Jess tagged along behind. The bizarre vision bothered him most because he wondered what he'd do with her once he got her there. With all his trust destroyed, he couldn't imagine them ever becoming the happy family he'd envisioned for so long. That was by far the worst part.

"Get out of my house," Sami ordered, her tears blurring the pitiless, harsh image of the sister who had just ruined her life.

"I'm going, I'm going," Vicki said. She'd started for the front door when Jess toddled into her path, rubbing his eyes with his chubby fists, whimpering, and obviously frightened.

He looked up at the lady in the funny, shiny clothes, his eyes wide, his face pale. "Where's my mama?"

"In there," Vicki said, pointing to the kitchen. She was totally taken aback by the strong family resemblance that had developed since the last time she'd seen Jess. All along she'd assumed it was an outside chance that Clay had actually fathered the child. Now, seeing how he'd grown and flourished, she had far fewer doubts. Their eyes, hair and facial expressions were strikingly similar. If Jess wasn't Clay's son, he sure as hell ought to be.

Trailing her sister to the door to make sure she left, Sami overheard the brief conversation. Teary-eyed, she bent down to take the scared little boy in her arms. "It's okay, honey. Mama's here."

"Somebody mad?"

Sami stroked his hair off his forehead and kissed him there. "Not now. Don't worry."

Jess looked up at her. "You cryin'?" He put his short arms around her neck as best he could. "Don't cry, Mama. I love you a whole bunch. Okay?"

"Okay, sweetheart." Picking him up and holding him close, she faced her sister. "You see how it is? I hope you realize what you've done to us."

"I haven't done anything to you."

"You know Clay will press this, somehow. He's a strong, decisive man who thinks he's been robbed of his son." A sob escaped from her constricted throat. "Oh, Vicki, what am I going to do?"

She shrugged. "Marry him, I guess. It's the simplest solution. He's not a bad husband. I just needed more variety and excitement in my life than one person could give me, that's all."

Sami gasped air in quick bursts, trying to calm herself enough to speak. "I will *never* marry."

"Why not?" Softening her defensive posture a bit, Vicki approached. "Judging by the sight of you with that kid, you were meant to be a wife and mother. So do it."

All inhibitions removed by the emotional shock she'd just undergone, Sami spoke her mind without hesitation. "You don't get it, do you? Do you remember anything about the last foster home we were in together?"

"It was the pits. So what? They got better after the county split us up."

"And do you have any idea why that happened?"

"Because you talked me into running away, I guess." Vicki made a sour face. "I never did see why all the cloak-

and-dagger stuff was necessary. What did it get us, except into more trouble?''

Sami clutched Jess tighter, stifled any lingering humiliation and managed to continue facing her sister. ''It got *you* away from the lowlife who abused me, for one.''

''What? You're nuts.''

''Am I? He told me it was my choice. Either I could submit to his advances or he'd start on you. As soon as I could scrape a few dollars together, I threw our clothes into a paper sack, took you by the hand and we ran off. The social workers didn't believe my explanation of what had happened, but I knew I'd done what I had to do, even if it meant we were separated for a while.''

''Oh, my God.''

''I *can't* get married,'' Sami said. ''Because that would mean I'd have to let a man make love to me, and I can't bear the idea, even now. I know. I've tried.''

''With Clay.''

''Yes.''

''Well, what did he say? I mean, he can be a pretty gentle guy when he wants to be. He'd take his time in bed if he knew you needed special treatment.''

''You think I *told* him?'' Sami stared unbelieving at the young woman she'd once rescued so gallantly. ''Since that first time, when I tried to sic the police on our foster father and the authorities looked at me like I was lying to cover my real reasons for running away, I haven't told this to another living soul.''

''Clay would believe you,'' Vicki assured her. ''I can see he loves you.'' She nodded toward Jess. ''The kid, too.''

''He did,'' Sami said. ''Now, thanks to you, he thinks I'm the worst liar in the history of the world.''

''He'll come around. You'll see. Once you guys are married, you can have other kids, like Jess, and he'll forget all about what happened today.''

Sami shook her head sadly. "No, Vicki. I won't have other children. Anyone's children." She placed a tender kiss on the top of her son's head and swayed back and forth to rock him.

"Why not?"

"You were just a kid but do you happen to remember when I kept going to one doctor after another because of female problems?"

"I guess so. Why?"

"They all said exactly what I'd been told for years. I can't conceive. Period. End of fairy tale. So you see why I could never agree to marry Clay even if I didn't have a hang-up about sex. He wants lots of children. He deserves a wife who can give them to him."

Vicki's jaw had dropped. Slowly, thoughtfully, she closed her mouth. "So that's why you made Jess the center of your life?"

"I love him. He's my son," Sami said. "He's all I have or ever will have."

"And I just blew it for you," Vicki whispered, coming closer. "Oh, God. I never understood, never dreamed how traumatic your life had been because of me. Aw, hell, Sami."

"It wasn't your fault. You were eight years old. We were just caught in a set of circumstances over which neither of us had any control."

Tears had begun to well in Vicki's eyes. "You'd protected me all along, and when you became my legal guardian, you were still doing it, weren't you? That's why you were so strict all the time."

"I tried not to be." She managed a fond smile. "You were one tough kid."

"And pretty dumb, it looks like." Vicki reached out a hand to cautiously pat her sister's arm. When Sami didn't jump back or swear at her, she inched an arm around her shoulders. "How can I ever say I'm sorry so you'll believe I really mean it?"

Sniffling, her lower lip trembling, Sami looked over at her. "I know you do." The moisture in her sister's eyes was liquefying the black lines rimming them and making her tears run a muddy gray down her cheeks. Sami took a finger and brushed some of the ugly wetness away. "You're a mess, sis."

Vicki let out a feeble, low chuckle and tried to blink back the rest of her tears while she swiped at the ones already on her face. "You try to blow my nose for me like you used to and you're history," she teased. "But I think we could both use a handful of tissues."

"There's a box on top of the refrigerator." Slowly, they started back to the kitchen together, Sami in the lead, Vicki's hand resting amiably on her shoulder.

"He really is a cute kid," Vicki said, peering sideways at Jess while he hid his face in the hollow of his mother's neck and shoulder.

"You think so?" No compliment could have pleased Sami more at that moment.

"Yeah. I guess I was just afraid I'd get too attached if I paid much attention to him. But don't worry. No matter what happens, he's still your baby. As far as I'm concerned, he always will be."

Sami seated herself at the table, Jess on her lap. "So what do we do now?"

"We wait for Clay to make his move, I guess," Vicki said. Placing the tissue box on the table between them, she pulled up the closest chair and sat down.

Sami handed her a tissue. "And we blow our noses."

Both women smiled at the ridiculousness of the simple, inane observation.

"We're a sight," Vicki said.

Nodding, Sami tenderly dried Jess's tears and then took care of what was left of her own. "You know, sis," she said, reaching over to pat Vicki's hand, "for once in our lives, I totally agree with you."

Chapter Ten

Sami had asked Vicki to stay over so they could talk longer, but since Mac and the SinSeers were still in town, the younger woman insisted on going home for the present.

"I have work to do, you know, a fresh manicure and such, but I'll be back," Vicki said, fanning out her fingers so she could inspect each crimson nail. "And Mac's been wanting me to have my hair dyed pink, like his."

"Mac has pink hair?" Sami raised an eyebrow as her sister giggled.

"You are so funny. Of course he has pink hair. It's his trademark. Haven't you seen pictures of the band?"

"Only in black and white, thank goodness. I'd probably have worried more than usual about his influence on you if I'd known he was so weird."

"He's not weird. It's an image," Vicki said. "Part of the job. Anyway, he's only going to stay pink till the European tour is over."

"You're going to Europe with him?"

"Yeah. France, England, Germany. Great, huh?" She bent down to give Jess a farewell kiss on his cheek. In the untutored, candid manner of small children, he made a face and wiped the spot with his hand, as if the touch of her lips had gotten him dirty.

Vicki laughed. "Oh, so you don't like kissing strange girls, huh? Well, get used to it, kid, because if you grow up to be half as cute as you are now, you'll have to beat them off with a stick."

Watching her sister depart, Sami was smiling as proudly as if she'd conceived and borne the delightful, precocious child herself. It was too bad Vicki couldn't have lingered longer.

Not that Sami minded a little peace and quiet for a change. From the first day that Clay had reappeared in her life, she hadn't been able to completely relax, nor had she had a decent night's sleep. That was probably why even the simplest task exhausted her to the point where she'd nod off simply reading bedtime stories to Jess, instead of the other way around.

Yawning, Sami trudged upstairs to her office and plunked down behind her computer. She'd have to get to work on the Elderhostel story before long, and then there was the human-interest piece about the man who raised bees in his backyard and gave the honey to the poor.

She stared at the bright blue screen of her monitor, her muzzy mind refusing to cooperate. Finally, she lowered her hands into her lap and looked down to be sure Jess was playing safely beside her on the floor. Her eyelids drooped, fluttered, then closed completely. Lord, she was beat. Just a few minutes' breather, she promised herself, then she'd get back to work.

When she next checked the time, almost an hour had passed and Jess was curled up in a fetal position, asleep, on the fleecy rose-colored rug beside her desk.

* * *

The fact that the approaching car was a silver sports car just like the one Clay had seen parked in Sami's driveway when he'd stormed out, tipped him off as to who had arrived. He cursed under his breath. He should have known better than to dally in Redlands when Vicki was around. She 'might be devious, but she was far from stupid.

"We have nothing to discuss," Clay said, when Vicki sought him out at the Sycamore building site. "You can leave your present address and telephone number with my secretary. My lawyers will handle our business dealings from now on."

"I didn't come on business," Vicki swore, drawing an invisible *X* with her finger across her heart. "I swear. I came to do you a favor."

He smirked. "Oh, good. I can hardly wait."

"Don't be an idiot, Clay. Sami loves you."

"If that's all you wanted to tell me, you're wasting your breath."

"I've done a lot of that lately," she said. "But this time, every word is worth listening to, believe me."

"I wouldn't believe you *or* your sister if my life depended on it," he shot back. Stalking away, he left her standing alone in the middle of the bare field.

She dogged his steps as well as she could across the hard, uneven ground. Her cumbersome, high-heeled boots offered little stability and she wound up extending her arms for balance like a circus tightrope walker.

"I don't blame you," Vicki called after him. "The thing is, I just found out some things about my big sister that make a tremendous difference to me and I can't imagine why they wouldn't affect you the same way."

"Forget it."

She half ran to keep up. "I can't. Sami was protecting me and I was too stupid to see it. I owe her." Making a futile grab for his arm, she added, "Damn it, Clay, she was abused as a kid!"

That brought him up short. "What?"

Breathing hard, Vicki bent over and rested her hands on her knees. "Thank goodness I finally got your attention."

"You have ten seconds to explain. Make it quick."

She stood erect and straightened the leather jumpsuit. "Okay. Here goes. I don't know the gory details, but everything Sami did, then and now, fits. Think about it—the running away, the overprotectiveness toward me, the way she never talked about certain stages of her teens, her aversion to having sex with anybody...."

"How do you know that part's true?"

"Because she just told me."

Unwilling to concede, he resumed walking. "Oh, sure. And you buy her story? No normal woman gets to her late twenties a virgin."

"I didn't say she was a *virgin*," Vicki shouted after him. "That's the problem."

Pausing, Clay took a few seconds to consider the possible validity of what Vicki was trying to convey. If there was even a remote chance Sami had been hurt like that, he couldn't just walk away from the knowledge. He turned and went back. "When did she say this all happened?"

Vicki shrugged. "I don't know exactly. She told me I was eight, so she must have been about sixteen. It was right before we ran away from the foster home."

"When Sami was removed from our local high school," he said quietly. "I remember how upset she seemed."

"Try scared to death. We had no parents or other close relatives, a bum had messed with her and threatened to do the same to me if she didn't submit, and our social worker refused to believe her accusations against the man. There she was, stuck in the middle of a no-win situation and hardly more than a kid herself."

Clay took a deep breath and stared off at the rolling hills and orange groves surrounding the development. As much as he wished he could dismiss Vicki's wild tale as a fabrication, he could see it might contain at least a modicum of fact. If Sami had been abused and had never sought professional treatment for the aftereffects, she was bound to be badly scarred.

"If what you say is true, it does explain a lot," he finally said. "Where is she now?"

"I left her at home and drove around looking for you. It was lucky I thought about the fact you might come here since you'd gotten me to fork over my piece of the action." She patted him on the forearm and smiled. "Well, the hard decisions are all yours now, big guy. I've gotta go. Mac's waiting for me."

Wobbling on her heels, she started off across the uneven field toward her car. Clay called after her, "Thanks," and she raised a hand to wave.

"Just promise you'll invite me to the wedding!"

Wedding? he thought, a wave of cynicism washing over him. What made Vicki think he still wanted to talk Sami into marrying him? Hell, after the past few hours, he wasn't sure he'd ever allow himself to believe any woman again.

Except for Sami, his heart added. Trying to argue against the thought and failing, Clay realized it was true. No matter what she'd said or done, he still loved her.

The nucleus of an idea began to develop in his mind. He'd spent years trying to break down the emotional barriers Sami had built, not even guessing what kind of horrible childhood demons she'd erected them against. No wonder his recent he-man approach had sent her into paroxysms of weeping. He cursed. There was no telling how many of her old scars he'd touched without dreaming he was hurting her.

At that moment, all Clay wanted to do was rush to her and gather her up in his arms, holding her safe against the past and carrying her with him into a happy future.

Only now he knew better than to try something overtly physical like that. Samantha Adamson was not a woman he could literally sweep off her feet the way he'd once dreamed of doing. Her bruised psyche was as fragile as eggshells, as sensitive as the newborn baby she'd rescued, and she'd have to be treated that way or he was afraid she'd never recover.

He climbed into the car and fastened his seat belt. Damned if he knew what he should do about Sami, but one thing was for sure—he was going to see to it she gave him an opportunity to show her that making love with him was nothing like the violent experience that had apparently damaged her trust so long ago.

All he needed was a fair chance. If she wouldn't willingly give it to him, well, he'd do whatever he had to and force the issue. In the end, she'd either hate him for it or understand why he'd pushed her so hard.

He *was* perfect for her, he assured himself. He always had been. Now all he had to do was convince Sami of that fact without alienating her for life.

Sending Jess out to play when he'd awakened from his nap, Sami found herself wandering aimlessly through the house. Serious concentration was impossible. So was minor concentration. No matter what she wanted to think about, her mind kept insisting she dwell on Clay and what might happen to Jess because of him. He'd never been a cruel or vindictive man. Then again, he'd never had his only son hidden from him for better than two years, either.

When she heard a knock at the front door, it didn't occur to her that there was the slightest chance her current caller might be Clay. Without a pause, she opened the door.

Seeing her, he smiled hopefully. "Hi." She was wearing an old sweatshirt, faded to a pale pink about the same shade as the leftover puffiness surrounding her eyes, he noted.

One look at Clay and she shut the door in his face.

He knocked again. "Sami? Come on. Let me in." There was no doubt he could have forced his way into the house, but considering the tale of horror he'd just heard, he refused to use physical means to gain his objective.

"Go away."

"Not till you hear what I have to say."

"Then I hope you have your car phone with you, because you'll be stuck out there so long you're going to have to send out for meals to keep from starving to death."

"I'll take my chances."

Leaning against the closed door, she moaned. "Don't you have a home?"

"Sure. I'll be glad to show it to you someday soon. How about tomorrow?" The unintelligible noise he heard in reply sounded something like "Aargh!" and he couldn't help but chuckle. Whether she knew it or not, Samantha Adamson was a naturally funny lady. No wonder keeping company with her had always been such a joy.

"Glad to hear it," Clay teased. "Well, I guess I'll have a seat on the glider here and bide my time. If your neighbor asks what I'm doing all by myself, I'll just tell her you threw me out and I'm waiting till hell freezes over for you to forgive me and let me back inside."

"That would be about right," Sami said.

"I figured as much."

Hearing no more from him, she waited as long as her curiosity permitted, then opened the door a crack to peek through. Clay was nowhere to be seen. His car, however, was still parked in the driveway. She stepped onto the wooden porch, looked up and down the block, then retreated.

Wherever he was, whatever game he was playing, he'd be back. She'd have bet the mortgage on it.

Wandering into the kitchen, she stood at the sink and checked on Jess through the window. Her heart, already overtaxed, did a feeble backflip and stuck in her throat, as usual.

Of course that was where Clay had gone. If her brain hadn't been as fuzzy as Jess's favorite teddy bear, she'd have figured out his plan sooner. Chances were excellent that from now on Clay Ellis would want to spend an inordinate amount of time with his son. That was normal. Sami wondered vaguely how long it was going to be before she fell apart entirely, from the strain of having to be near him merely because Jess was.

Clay was getting to his feet and speaking to the little boy now, she noted, not terribly surprised when he left the toddler happily at play and headed for the kitchen door.

Letting himself in, he paused by the entrance. "May I?"

Sami shrugged. "You're in. You might as well stay in." It was as if her emotions had somehow been disconnected from what was going on in her surroundings. She felt a certain amount of uneasiness, but nothing like the degree of nervousness Clay's presence usually triggered.

Walking to the table, she sat down heavily. "I suppose you've come to deliver an ultimatum."

"In a way," he said, her marked depression helping him take the final step in his mind. "I've come to ask you to marry me."

She managed a short, disparaging laugh.

"I'm serious, Sami." Clay approached the table. "Marry me."

"Or what?" she asked, unable to believe he had no hidden agenda to go along with the proposal.

Moving purposefully, he seated himself across from her and placed his hand lightly atop hers. "Or I will be forced to start legal proceedings to claim my son." The tears which gathered in her already reddened eyes tore his heart apart, but he held his real response in check. If the only way to reach her was through her love for Jess, then so be it.

Sami studied his face for a long time. "You mean that, don't you?"

"Yes."

"And if I refuse to marry you?"

"I already told you what I'd do. You don't have a choice. We can do this the easy way or the hard way. If you want to continue to be Jess's mother, then you're going to have to let me become his father."

Biting her lower lip, she decided to give him the best reason she could think of to reject her. After baring her soul to Vicki, the idea of telling the disgusting story a second time seemed far less inconceivable.

"I'm not the person you think I am," she said slowly, clearly. "There are things in my past I'm ashamed of."

"You mean what happened to you when you were sixteen?"

Sami's jaw dropped. "You know? How?"

"Vicki," Clay said.

"She had no right!"

Stroking the back of her hand, he tried to soothe her. "Your sister was just trying to pay you back for all you did for her," he said. "None of us realized what hell you had gone through." His vision clouded. "Damn it, Sami, we were friends. Why didn't you confide in me?"

"Why? So you could condemn me like all the others? You don't want to marry me, Clay."

"Yes, I do."

"Because of Jess," she said, nodding. "I can understand that. But you don't have to take me, too, in order to insure yourself a permanent place in his life. You can visit him here or invite him to your house anytime you want. I'll put it in writing, if necessary."

Clay shook his head. "I'm afraid that won't do, Sami. You and I are getting married."

"No, Clay."

"Yes, Samantha. I think the Methodist church where we used to go to Sunday School would be the best place to have the service. Do you want to make the arrangements with Pastor Sorenson, or shall I?"

This should have been the happiest moment of her life, she thought sadly, yet here she was, listening to the man she loved talk about their wedding and feeling surprisingly little emotional involvement. It was as if her spirit had finally been numbed beyond its ability to recover.

She barely saw Clay when she looked his way. *I suppose I ought to be glad he's offering to let me keep Jess*, she thought. That was the only really important fact. The rest of her life was already a shambles. A loveless marriage wouldn't make it that much worse, and if she couldn't bring herself to sleep with Clay as man and wife, then he'd just have to live with her decision. It wasn't as if he hadn't been warned.

"All right, Clay, I'll marry you," she said, thrusting out her chin. "But I won't be rushed. As a little girl, I dreamed of walking down the aisle in a flowing white gown. Maybe I don't deserve to wear white because of my past, but I intend to have that dress. And bridesmaids."

He nodded. "Since your father's gone, Jess can be your escort, if you want. That way he'll feel like he's an important part of what's happening."

"How long will you give me to prepare?" She had no idea how much planning went into most ceremonies, but with her organizational skills, she figured she could handle any constraints he placed on her.

"How long do you want?"

His easy acquiescence amazed her. "Is two months too long?" Sami would have asked for more time if she'd thought Clay would agree. Things were going so well for her so far, she decided she shouldn't push her luck.

Two *hours* is too long, Clay thought, but at least they'd gotten past her flat refusal. "That will be fine." He glanced at the back door. "Shall we go tell Jess?"

Getting to her feet, Sami sighed. "I suppose we might as well. He's so inquisitive he'll figure out something's up, anyway, and drive me crazy till I admit I have a secret."

"Takes after me," Clay said. "I never could pass up a good puzzle." As she walked past him, he started to reach for her, then stopped. "Sami?"

"Yes?" She turned to him.

"Can I kiss you?"

The fractious butterflies were back in her stomach in an instant. However, she also realized his request wasn't out of line. If they were to be husband and wife, she supposed he'd expect her to act the part, at least to the extent she was able.

Nodding consent, she stepped closer to him and felt his arms close around her. His body was warm, comforting, and she let herself sink into the sensation till Clay was all that filled her mind and soul.

She lifted her face, her lips parted, trembling, and the tender glow between them increased, encompassing their bodies and rendering them one in spirit. He kissed her then, the slow, sensuous movement of his mouth on hers barely perceptible.

Sami pressed closer. If only making love were this romantic, she mused, then she'd be happy forever. The errant thought almost caused her to break contact with Clay, but she managed to override the irrational impulse.

Her eyes open, she concentrated on his dear face, the kindness and compassion in his eyes, the sensation of his breath as it traveled softly across her skin in tingling waves.

Clay cupped her cheeks in his hands and gazed down at her. "It will be good for us, Sami. I promise you it will."

Assuming Vicki had also told him she could never bear him children, Sami wondered how he had managed to change his personal goals and alter his outlook on life so rapidly.

"Come on," he said, taking her hand and urging her along. "We have a little boy to surprise with some terrific news."

Pensive, Sami followed. Clay was a good man. He'd make an excellent father for Jess. She'd go ahead and plan her wedding, as promised, but in the back of her mind she couldn't help but hope he'd change his mind about coercing her into it—before it was too late for both of them.

Chapter Eleven

It seemed to Sami, as the weeks passed, that Clay was barely aware she existed. Oh, he was friendly and solicitous if she needed something repaired around the house or inquired about his choices regarding their upcoming wedding, but he didn't go to any trouble to be alone with her.

In a way, her concerns were laughable. She was the one who had worried about fielding his sexual advances, and now here she was, fretting about their absence.

During Clay's frequent visits to see Jess, Sami often found herself recalling episodes from her own early childhood. Actually, she mused, they weren't always precisely incidents, sometimes they were more feelings or impressions of what life had been like back then. It was obvious Clay's presence was triggering her faded memory of her parents and their family's interactions, and Sami wasn't too sure she liked remembering all that much.

A month before the wedding, Clay had casually re-

arked about Vicki's basic character, and Sami's mind had
ashed vividly back to the early days of her sister's life.

Mother hadn't been feeling well for some time and had
nally been taken to the hospital. Sami remembered pray-
g fervently and weeping for her mother's safe return, only
▪ learn that she wasn't sick, after all. The tiny, wizened
undle her parents had brought home was not only a sur-
rise to Sami, it turned out to be more trouble than it was
orth.

"Don't touch the baby," Mother had warned. "She's
uch too delicate."

Her father had at least paused long enough to pat Sami
n the head before joining in the sickening fawning over the
ew arrival.

"Can I hold her?" Sami thought her mother was going
▪ slap her for asking.

"No! Don't you dare try, you stupid girl."

"Now, Norma," Father had said, "Samantha was just
retending. Weren't you, dear? She wouldn't dream of
othering her baby sister." He'd smiled then, his eyes not
early as happy as Sami liked to see them.

Curiosity about the baby had brought Sami tiptoeing to
eek into her crib more than once those first few months. As
icki got older, her physical loveliness grew. So did her
mper. Their parents had coddled the younger sister and
ut up with her tantrums, while Sami had developed a
rong sense of responsibility and self-reliance on her own.

She and Vicki were as close as such wildly differing per-
nalities could be, she supposed, and in a way, she proba-
y did owe some of her character strengths to the fact she'd
t ignored and had had to fend for herself so much of the
ne. Funny how things worked out, wasn't it?

And now they were truly friends, Sami thought with a tug
emotion. Vicki stayed away whenever Clay was around,

which was almost all the time, but they did often talk for hours on the telephone.

Remembering that it was only a few more days till Mac and his entourage left for Europe, Sami picked up the phone and dialed her sister's number. A member of the band answered, then passed the phone to Vicki.

"*Bon jour,*" Vicki said, giggling. "I'm trying to learn French. It's the pits. How are you?"

"Pretty good, considering."

"He's there again?"

Sami made a guttural sound of disgust. "Of course. Where else would he be?"

"Working. We all have to work once in a while to pay for our life-styles. At least, that's what Mac says."

"Clay has moved a trailer onto the Sycamore development site and he sleeps there. That way, he gains two hours he wouldn't have free if he tried to drive back and forth to his place in Victorville every day."

"Smart. You should be impressed."

"Oh, yeah. I'm ecstatic. Of course, I haven't gotten a single newspaper article properly polished since three weeks ago when he started this nonsense."

"Doesn't he watch Jess for you so you can write?"

Sami had to admit her sister had a valid point. "Yes, he does. The problem is, they have so much fun and make so much racket, I can't concentrate."

Vicki giggled again. "I don't suppose it's occurred to you to join them?"

"It's occurred to me."

"But you haven't done it."

"Bingo. You get the prize for the right answer."

"Still avoiding Clay?" Vicki asked. The pitch of her voice told Sami she didn't approve.

"I know you won't believe this, but it hasn't been a problem. Clay seems determined to avoid me instead. When we do speak, it's usually about Jess or the house or our careers." Sami sighed. "I had all these wonderful excuses stored up for whenever he made a move on me, and he hasn't done a thing that would make me need them."

"Oh, God," Vicki said. "You two sound *married!*"

"Actually, I'd made the same comparison some time ago. It's not all bad, you know. I am feeling a lot more relaxed around him."

"Brides are not supposed to feel relaxed, Sami. You're supposed to be on fire for the guy. Hot to trot. So turned on you can't keep your hands off him." She paused to lower her voice and cup the receiver with her hand. "Go see a shrink before the wedding, sis. Try to get your head on straight before you marry Clay, or you're liable to lose him."

More resigned to her fate each day, Sami shook her head slowly from side to side. "No. There's not a chance of that happening. I've told you before, Clay is only doing this because of Jess."

"I can't believe you really think that."

"I don't think it—I know it. He's said it over and over in a lot of different ways. He's saying it right now by spending all his time with Jess and treating me like I hardly matter, except where my son is concerned."

"I think you're wrong," Vicki insisted. "Clay is a sensitive guy. Maybe you need to let him know it's all right with you if he makes a pass or two."

"It's *not* all right with me," Sami said. "I like him just fine the way he is."

"Boring?"

"Blasé. Detached. Even a little distant. It makes it much easier for me to cope with his hanging around here all the time."

"Aha! He *does* bother you! I knew it."

Sami was sorry her sister couldn't see the sour face she was making. "Bon voyage, Vicki. Go to Paris, or wherever, and lecture the French about interpersonal relationships instead of always telling me what to do, will you?"

"Just paying you back for all those years you played my mama," the younger woman said. "By the way, I'm off drugs and booze. Thought you'd like to know."

That was the best news Sami had heard in months. "Oh, honey. I'm so glad."

"Knew you would be. Kiss the brat for me." She laughed with genuine affection in her voice. "Kiss his dear ol' daddy, too, if you dare! Ta-ta."

Sami was smiling as she hung up the receiver. Once she and her sister had stopped fighting, they'd found true camaraderie was easier than either of them had dreamed.

Lost in her reverie, she jumped at the sound of a deep voice directly behind her.

"How is Vicki?" Clay asked.

Sami's hand came to rest on the telephone, as if to magically guard the content of their prior conversation from him. "Fine. She says she's clean. No more self-destructive behavior. I hope she sticks with it."

"So do I," he said, nodding gravely. "Anything else new?"

"Not really. Why?" She had the uneasy feeling Clay may have overheard more of their sisterly exchange than he was letting on.

He shrugged. "No reason. Jess says he wants to go out for pizza tonight, and I promised him I'd ask you to come with us. How about it?"

"Tonight?" Sami felt her palms growing clammy, her mouth unusually dry. "I should work. But you two go ahead. I don't mind grabbing a bite to eat here." She thoroughly expected him to argue, to plead with her for her company, maybe even to threaten. When he merely stuffed his hands into his pockets, nodded and turned to walk away, she noticed a definite psychological letdown.

This is idiotic, she told herself. *He gave me precisely what I asked for. I have no reason to be disappointed.* But she was. Terribly. Once again, Clay's actions were contrary to what she'd come to expect from him in the past. It was as if he'd written her off, as if she no longer mattered to him at all.

That wasn't what she'd planned when she'd confided in him one evening right after they'd become engaged. Clay had presented her with a beautiful sapphire-and-diamond ring, and under the circumstances, she had felt it was only fair to make it clear to him that she wasn't ready for a physical relationship.

On the other hand, Clay had indicated he was more than ready, so perhaps his apparent change of heart was for the best. What he didn't demand, she didn't have to refuse to give.

The trouble was, Sami would have liked to at least be *asked*, even though she intended to turn him down flat.

Clay hired a crew to clean and paint the old Victorian house before the wedding, in spite of Sami's mild objections.

"It's silly to spend so much to refurbish this place if we're not going to live here," she argued.

"We may as well keep it up. Besides, don't you want it to look nice for the reception?" Clay spoke briefly with the painters, then returned to her. "I'm having it done over in the same colors, if that's all right with you."

"The color is fine. I just don't think you should have to pay the bills for my house, and I can't afford to lay out that much cash right now."

"It will be *our* house in a few weeks, Sami. Which reminds me. You haven't told me what changes you want made in the place in Victorville."

"I don't want to make any changes," she said. "That's your house and you furnished it to suit your tastes. It should stay like it is."

He placed his hands lightly on her shoulders. "Samantha. I'm an old-fashioned guy. What's mine is yours, and vice versa, okay?"

"Okay." This was the first time since the night of their engagement that Clay had actually touched her, and she began to tremble with the thought, the heady anticipation that he was finally going to kiss her again.

Instead he withdrew, leaving her standing there staring after him and wondering what she'd said or done to make him pull away.

He approached the familiar men in the painting crew and leaned against the back of their truck. John and Andy had worked for him, on and off, for the past six or seven years. "The off-white siding and blue trim is fine with her," Clay said. "Go ahead and get started." Fighting a headache, he pinched the bridge of his nose with thumb and forefinger.

John reached for his paint-splattered coveralls and stepped into them. "Sure, boss. Anybody tell you lately you look like hell?"

"Several people." Clay muttered a curse. "I'm having a devil of a time keeping my hands off that woman. Just being in the same room with her makes me crazy."

"So go ahead and sleep with her." The painter zipped up the coveralls as he cast a leer in Sami's direction. "She doesn't look like she'd mind a little extra lovin' on the side."

Clay had John by the collar and hauled up against the side of the truck before the man could duck. Andy made himself scarce. "If I ever hear you talk like that about her again, I'll see you never get another contract for one of my projects. Clear?"

"Hey. Okay. No offense meant," John said, his face reddening. "You want to wait till you're married, that's fine with me. Only don't break my neck because you're mad you're not getting any, okay?"

The man had a valid point. Clay lowered him to the ground and straightened his rumpled collar for him. "Sorry. Maybe I am a little strung out by all this. Just paint the damn house, stay away from my future wife in the process, and I'll be happy."

"You got it, boss."

Clay walked slowly back to the old house and climbed the steps onto the porch, pausing to look around. He'd taken down the glider so it wouldn't be in the workmen's way, and he missed the old swing already. Someday he and Sami would sit together on it, share sweet, tender kisses and maybe even make love there, under a blanket, on a moonless night.

He felt the readiness of his body. This was getting ridiculous. One errant thought and he was primed again. If there was anything left of his rampant sexual desire by the time he and Sami were actually married, he'd have to tread very softly around her. Maybe even more than he had been. For *both* their sakes.

Reminding himself that he must not frighten or hurt her no matter what, he managed to wrestle his fractious libido into at least a semblance of submission. The past weeks had been holy hell on his self-control, but Clay knew they were nothing compared to the trial he would soon face.

If he hadn't loved Sami with such total allegiance, such complete commitment, he was certain he'd never have been able to stand the pressure.

Sami would have made Vicki her matron of honor if she hadn't been on her way from Paris to Copenhagen with Mac and his band by the time the date of the nuptials rolled around.

Eleanor Truesdale was the most logical second choice, and since their children were such good friends, Sami managed to include all of them, too, in one capacity or another. That was a good thing, because Eleanor wound up making all the girl's outfits herself.

"I don't know what I'd have done if you weren't such a wonderful seamstress," Sami told her one evening while helping to hem Tiffany's bridesmaid's gown. "I couldn't believe the bridal shop wanted these dresses ordered six months in advance!"

"We were lucky to find all the fabric on sale," Eleanor said. "I love these fall colors, don't you?"

"I'd better. I chose them." Sami smiled over at the smaller finished garment hanging on a folding rack in Eleanor's sewing room. "Has Tricia finally gotten over the trauma of having to wear a dress exactly like her sister's?"

"She'll live. I told her, it's *your* wedding, not hers, and putting it in that perspective helped, I think." Biting off a thread, she shook out the bodice she'd been basting together. "Have you had Jess fitted for his tux yet?"

Sami chuckled. "Yesterday. He looked darling!"

"As darling as his daddy?" She shook her head and pursed her lips. "You should have told me, you know. I never would have dumped Jess on your doorstep that day if I'd known what you were up to."

"I know. It just seemed better to keep everything to myself. If I had it to do over again, I'd probably ask you to help me keep my secret about Jess's natural mother and father."

"And miss your big chance to marry Clay?" Eleanor whistled between her teeth. "Boy, it looks like you and I need to have a serious mother-daughter talk!"

"Just *sew*, Mrs. Truesdale," Sami quipped. "I don't want to talk about the birds and the bees."

"How about the girls and the boys?"

"Them, either." Sami laughed softly. "I get quite enough of that from my son. Thanks to Clay, he's discovered the major differences between men and women, and delights in telling everyone we meet."

She tittered. "I know. He filled me in last week."

"Eesh. Sorry."

"No problem. Bennie got quite a chuckle out of it, too, especially when Jess asked to see *his.* "

"Oh, boy. Let's change the subject, shall we?"

"Sure. Tell me more about the dress you found for yourself. I'll bet it's gorgeous."

"It is pretty," Sami said. "It has a lace bodice with seed pearls, a scalloped neckline, a fitted, dropped waist and a train. I loved it the minute I saw it. There were only two dresses in my size in the whole store and that one was on sale. Good thing, too. I had no idea how much all this was going to cost or I'd have suggested Clay and I run off to Vegas to get married."

"Why didn't you?"

Sami wasn't about to admit her first thought had been to stall him in the hopes he'd change his mind. By the time she'd realized he wasn't going to waver, they were financially committed in regard to most of the necessary components of the wedding. Besides, she did like the idea of holding the ceremony in the church where they'd often met as children.

"I don't know why Vegas never came up," Sami alibied. "I guess I wasn't thinking too clearly when he asked me to marry him."

Eleanor laughed loudly. "Now, *that's* the first completely logical thing you've said in a long time. I'd be dithered, too, if a hunk like your Clay asked me to marry him. He's a great father—even Bennie said so, and he's hard to impress."

"Really?"

"No fooling. After you and Clay get back from your honeymoon, don't be a stranger, okay? We'll plan a barbecue in the backyard or something."

"Honeymoon? I hadn't thought much about going away anywhere, but I suppose Clay will want to." She hoped he'd postpone any trips for the sake of his shopping-center project and at least give her a chance to get used to being married to him first.

"Of course you'll go somewhere special. He's already shown he spares no expense where you're concerned. Take that ring..." She eyed the sparkling blue-and-white creation on Sami's left hand. "Wow!"

Twisting it around her finger, Sami grew thoughtful. The past few weeks had seemed like little more than a bizarre dream. Once in a while, like now when Eleanor brought up honeymoons, Sami received a jolt of reality, but for the most part she was a dreamer caught in a vortex of wild imaginings. This couldn't be true. She couldn't actually be engaged to marry Clay. The idea was so farfetched it was nearly impossible to comprehend.

Chapter Twelve

Tricia and Tiffany made beautiful junior bridesmaids in their burgundy-and-dusty-rose gowns. Sporting matching miniature tuxedos, Tommy was an usher and Travis the ring-bearer. Because Jess was walking his mother down the aisle, he didn't seem to mind the parts the other children had in the ceremony.

For best man, Clay had picked Dick Rasmussen, the detective who had tracked down Jess's birth records. He hadn't actually asked him to stand up with him, though, until he'd cleared the choice with Sami. Touched by Clay's sensitivity and concern for her feelings, she'd readily agreed.

The autumn day dawned bright and crisp, with a high temperature expected in the low seventies. Until that morning, Sami hadn't experienced much nervousness. Actually, she hadn't let herself dwell for long on what lay beyond the ceremony, so she had managed to forestall the eventual acknowledgment of her innermost fears.

That all ended when she awoke on *the* day. What had begun as a mild uneasiness had escalated into near panic by early afternoon. Staring at her pale image in the mirror in the church dressing room, she wondered how in heaven's name she'd gotten there. The question was ridiculous, of course, but that didn't keep her from asking it, over and over, and coming up with no lucid answer whatsoever.

"You look *beautiful,*" Eleanor gushed, admiring the old-fashioned lace-and-satin creation with its sweeping train and hand-embroidered pearl accents. "You're right. That dress is the prettiest I've ever seen. I wish *my* waist was that tiny."

Sami touched the single string of pearls at her neck. "Thank you for loaning me these. They're perfect."

"Well, something borrowed."

"Besides the groom, you mean?"

Making a silly face, Eleanor adjusted Sami's veil for the third time. "I thought you and your sister had settled all that."

"We have." Sami shrugged. "I wish she could be here today, but she was afraid to let Mac out of her sight long enough to fly back and forth from Denmark."

"You certainly won't have worries like that with your new husband," the older woman offered. "Anyone can see he's madly in love."

With his son, Sami thought. If it weren't for Jess, neither of them would be standing at the altar in a little while, promising to love, honor and cherish.

She glanced at the chair in the corner where Travis Truesdale was trying to tie Jess's black patent leather shoes with lots of unwanted coaching from Tricia, Tiffany and Tommy. Judging by the commotion, it was a good thing their mother was in the room.

Eleanor raised her voice only once and the bedlam ceased. "I warned them I'd send them out to sit in the pew with their father if they didn't behave," she explained. "It worked like a charm. You have no idea how excited they all were about this day."

Sami's eyes rolled, her eyebrows arching. "Oh, I'll bet I do."

"You're doing the right thing," the older woman said. "Married life is great with the right man. I know." She giggled. "You're looking at some of the benefits right now, although kids are not the only good part. How many more do you and Clay expect to have?"

"What?" Sami hadn't been listening too closely to what her friend was saying and was just now tuning in.

"Children. I was chatting with Clay the other day and he sounded like my Bennie—all excited about filling every bedroom in that big house of his."

Sami felt as if a huge fist had clamped around her heart. Suddenly she knew what had been bothering her, lingering at the fringes of her subconscious and refusing to come to the fore for the past two months.

She pushed back her veil and thrust her bouquet at Eleanor. "Here. Hold this. I'll be right back."

"But..."

Catching up her train by the wrist loop and gathering it close, Sami was out the dressing room door and halfway down the adjoining hall before her friend recovered and called after her.

Organ music reverberated as she negotiated the narrow, slightly musty corridor, the hem of her full skirt brushing against the walls as it swung from side to side. Her current journey reminded her of the days when she and Vicki had joined the children's choir for a season and played hide-and-seek behind the scenes with the other children.

The church sanctuary had been remodeled at least once since then, but fortunately the old behind-the-scenes passageways hadn't changed. It was still possible for Sami to reach Clay without any of their guests seeing her do it.

Frantic by the time she reached the closed door to the pastor's study, which temporarily served as the men's dressing room, she rapped violently.

Gray-haired, grandfatherly Pastor Sorenson answered, his ready smile turning to surprise. "Samantha! You belong at the other end of the church."

"I know." She jockeyed to peer into the room past his black-robed shoulder. "But I have to see Clay."

"Be patient, and in a few more minutes you'll get to see him anytime you want for the rest of your life."

"No! Now! I have to talk to him *now*."

Hearing the distress in her voice, Clay elbowed past, took her arm and led her back out into the hall, shutting the door behind them for privacy. "Calm down, Sami. What is it? What's wrong? Is Jess all right? He's not scared, is he?"

"No. Just be quiet a minute, will you?" She paused to try to catch her breath. The fist still clutched her heart like iron and Clay's handsome looks weren't helping. His tuxedo fit as if it had been tailored expressly for him, accentuating his broad shoulders, narrow waist and athletic body. If he'd been standing before her stark naked, he couldn't have appealed to her any more.

Sami took a deep, shuddering breath. "I want to know exactly what my sister told you about my awful past."

"Now? Here?"

"Yes. Believe me, I have my reasons."

"I'm sure you think you do," Clay said, "but I'm not about to drag all those old memories into the present on a day like this. Let it go, Sami. It's over. Done. Think about our future, not something you can't change."

"What I can't change is what's wrong with our future," she said, watching his face for any sign of negative emotion. "I have to be certain you understand everything about me before we go through with this."

"I've already agreed to marry you and I don't intend to change my mind, no matter what you say," he countered. "All that's left is the formality of the ceremony."

"But what about children?" she asked. The quizzical look on his face confirmed her worst fears. "You don't know, do you?"

"Know what?" Sensing her need for someone steady to lean on, he lightly took her arm.

"I can't have children," she said, her voice quavering.

"What are you talking about?"

Sami jerked her arm free from his loose grasp and squared her shoulders. "When you told me you and Vicki had discussed my problems, I assumed she'd told you *everything* about me. A few minutes ago, talking to Eleanor, it occurred to me that it was likely my scatterbrained sister had left out an important fact. That's why I had to see you before it was too late—to release you from your promise." She knew her rapid-fire babbling was nearly incoherent, but she couldn't help herself.

"Don't be ridiculous."

"I'm not the one who's being ridiculous. You always told me how much you wanted a big family. That was one of the reasons I left town when I did. You kept going on and on about kids, and I already knew I couldn't conceive."

Running a hand over the back of his neck, he shook his head. "After all the time we've had to discuss this, you waited till now to spring it on me? Why?"

"Because I don't want you to go through with our marriage if a big family is still what you want. No one will blame you for backing out, least of all me."

Sobering, Clay straightened the jacket of his tuxedo while he considered what Sami had just revealed. It was obvious how upset she was. The question was, did the desperation in her demeanor come about because she was telling him an outright lie or because the truth was so painful? Either way, he decided, the disclosure didn't change his plans the way she'd apparently thought it would.

He shook his head in the negative. "It won't work, Sami. Don't expect me to turn tail and run after all I've gone through to get you to the church. Go on back to your bridesmaids. You and I are due at the altar."

"Please, Clay," she begged, "you have to believe me."

"Whether I do or not doesn't matter," he said. "By the end of this afternoon, I expect to be Jess's official daddy. That's just how it is." Turning, he reentered the pastor's study and shut her out.

Sami slowly made her way back down the hall. She'd done all she could to warn Clay, to be fair to him, and he'd acted as if she'd made the whole thing up. For a person like her, whose moral principles were based on honesty and integrity, that was a hard judgment to accept.

It had been just as hard to take when the social worker had refused to act on her accusation of abuse all those years ago, she mused. No matter how much time passed, some things never changed, did they?

She heard the opening strains of Wagner's wedding march from *Lohengrin*. That was her cue. The hour had come when she would become Mrs. Clay Ellis in front of a small assembly of their closest friends and the pastor who had baptized them both as youngsters.

Turning the corner into the narthex, she joined a relieved Eleanor Truesdale and reclaimed her bride's bouquet while the older woman fixed her veil for her.

"Where were you?" Eleanor whispered.

"I took a short trip to hell," Sami said, blinking back tears of frustration. Thankfully, there was no more time for conversation. The first part of the procession started down the long aisle while the church-wedding coordinator spread Sami's train behind her and led Jess into place at her side. Hand in hand, mother and son stepped forward.

Pink and yellow rose petals carpeted their path, candles glowed on the altar, sprays of white roses and gladiolus pears framed each side of the latticework arch where she and Clay would take their vows. Immediately behind it, at the far end of the sanctuary, a stained-glass window cast rainbows of shimmering light on the consecrated site.

Sami gazed down lovingly at Jess and knew that no matter what else happened, what eventual trials she had to endure, what sacrifices she had to make, she was doing the right thing for her son. That was as it should be. Clay might be his father, but *she* was his mother. Putting his happiness ahead of her own was her solemn duty.

If Sami had been told she could lay claim to a million dollars by simply relating a detailed account of her wedding to Clay, she would have had to forfeit the money. In a haze, she went through the appropriate motions, hearing and seeing little. Jess had fussed once and Eleanor's brood had taken care of his needs. Other than that, Sami had been oblivious.

Clay had hired a professional photographer, insisting they treat their nuptials like any other couple would. As husband and wife, she and Clay had posed, briefly kissed, smiled and acted like normal newlyweds, yet in Sami's mind, a stranger was going through the farcical performance in her place.

Thankfully, the assemblage was confined to a group of their closest friends. While Jess ran around the room playing tag with the Truesdale brood, Sami shook hands and accepted kisses and good wishes till everyone seemed satisfied.

She knew her small talk was repetitive and bland, but with her mind spinning out of control the way it was, she figured she was lucky to remember her own name. Which had just changed, she was reminded by the next person to approach.

"Mr. and Mrs. Ellis," Pastor Sorenson said, shaking Clay's hand and holding Sami's the tender way her father used to when he was alive. "My Helga always did predict you two would get together someday."

"So did I," Clay said. He looked at his new wife. Her skin was pale, her cheeks flushed. Slipping his arm around her waist, he gave her a brief, supportive hug. "We'd be pleased if you and Helga could come to Sami's for a little get-together this evening around six. It won't be fancy. Just some old friends."

The clergyman grinned broadly. "We'd love to. Shall we bring a dish?"

"Thanks. That won't be necessary," Clay told him. "I've arranged for a caterer."

"At six, then." He placed a congratulatory kiss on Sami's cheek. "God bless you both."

Clay turned to her as soon as they were ostensibly alone. "Are you all right?"

"I guess so. Why?"

"I don't know. You look kind of funny. How about a glass of punch?" Trying to get her to smile, he added, "It's *not* homemade lemonade."

"Fine. Whatever you say."

Scowling, he paused a moment, then left to get her drink. By the time he returned, she'd seated herself in a folding chair and let Jess climb onto her lap. He was fiddling with the pearls on her dress, pretending to count them and getting all the way to three before starting over again.

"Maybe you'd better stand up," Clay said. "This red stuff looks like it might stain if it spilled."

"It doesn't matter," Sami said. Accepting the clear plastic cup, she gave Jess a sip before tasting it herself.

"You mean, *nothing* matters, don't you?" Clay guessed.

"Whatever you say. You're the boss."

"I didn't marry you to be anybody's boss," he countered. "I married you because I love you—and Jess."

"But you still don't trust me," Sami said quietly, sadly. "I tried to tell you the truth before it was too late, and you treated me like it was all a ploy on my part to get out of marrying you." She fought the tears of disappointment forming in her eyes and wetting her lashes.

Puzzled, Clay stared at her. "What are you talking about?"

"Children," Sami said, hugging Jess to her and kissing his forehead in spite of his struggles to lean back and continue counting seed pearls. "Maybe you'll believe me now that you can see I have nothing to gain. I've been to numerous doctors and specialists, Clay. Married to me, your family will consist of one child only, and you're looking at him."

He pulled a folding chair closer to her and sat down. Removing Jess from her lap and sending him off to chase Tommy and Travis, he took Sami's hands in his. "It'll be all right, honey. Don't worry about more kids now. I know you're disappointed in what the doctors said, but don't let it get you down."

Shaking her head, Sami laughed softly, cynically. "It isn't the medical profession or their tough diagnosis I'm disappointed in, Clay. It's you."

"Me? What did I do?"

"You doubted my confession and insisted we go ahead with the wedding, when what I needed was to see that you believed in me enough to take the decision whether or not to marry me seriously. You may think you've forgiven Vicki and me for deceiving you about Jess, but you haven't."

"Is that why you've been sulking?" he asked, unconscious indignation tingeing his words.

Sami sighed, blotted a stray tear off her cheek with a lace handkerchief and stood. "I haven't been sulking, Clay. To tell you the truth—for the *second* time today—I don't feel much of anything anymore. We're married, like you wanted, and you're now in the official position of Jess's father. What more do you want?"

Love, he wanted to say. *Your love, like we both know it should be.* Instead, he took her elbow and led her to the table where their cake waited to be cut.

They stood together, knife in hand. "Smile, Samantha," Clay whispered in her ear. "Look happy, or people might begin to wonder why you married me."

She managed a brave, brief grin that lasted long enough for the photographer to capture it on film. Everyone else, even Clay, looked so joyful, so at peace. This was her wedding day. It seemed monumentally unfair to Sami that her heart was the only one that was broken.

Eleanor had dashed home with Bennie and the kids to see to it they all changed out of their finery and settled down before going over to Sami's. When the newlyweds arrived, honking the horn of Clay's pom-pom- and streamer-decorated Beemer, she happily informed Sami that she'd arranged to also take Jess off her hands for the remainder of the afternoon.

"His play clothes are already at my house," she said. "You two need a little time to yourselves. I'll bring him back in a couple of hours, when I see the catering truck."

"That won't be necessary," Sami insisted. "Really. Jess can stay here and keep us company."

"Nonsense." Already halfway across the lawn with the toddler in tow, she didn't hesitate or look back.

Sami glanced at Clay. He'd been taking in the incident without comment or expression. Though they were now alone, his present demeanor gave no indication of how he felt, either.

She, on the other hand, was not thrilled with Eleanor's well-intentioned interference. Given her way, Sami would have kept her son by her side indefinitely as a handy buffer against intimacy. Going inside the empty house with Clay wasn't high on her list of priorities. However, they also couldn't remain out on the front lawn in formal clothing for too long without attracting undue attention.

She looked around, surprised to find she was standing there alone. Clay had evidently already come to the same conclusion about getting off the street as she had, since he was unlocking the front door.

Sami hoisted her long skirt and followed silently. No matter how mad he got, she was *not* going to cave in to his demands just because he was now her husband. He could rant and rave all he wanted—it wouldn't buy him any favors from her that she didn't want to give.

Swinging the train of her gown over her arm to keep it up off the ground, she hesitated a few moments to gather her courage, then climbed the porch steps and entered the house well after Clay. Once they were alone, behind closed doors, she was certain he'd want to have sex. Well, if he thought she was going to concede to his demands in private the way she had in public every time he spoke, he was dead wrong.

Sami closed the door behind her and took in the vacant entryway, then peered sideways down the hall toward the kitchen, wary of encountering Clay. The minute he confronted her, she was going to tell him exactly what she thought of him and his coercion. He may have forced her to marry him for Jess's sake, but that was where his influence ended.

No lawyer or detective or whoever else he decided to sic on her was going to make her budge, either. What went on when it was just the two of them was his word against hers.

He could yell and scream about conjugal rights all day and all night if he wanted—she didn't care. She was *not* going to bed with him and that was that.

Quieting her thoughts, Sami listened to the creaks and groans that were typical of the old house. Clay could be plainly heard moving around upstairs. Probably getting the master bedroom ready for an orgy, she thought nervously. Okay. She wasn't afraid of him, nor was she going to tiptoe around in her own house simply because he also happened to be present. If he wanted to have it out with her up there instead of on the ground floor, then she was ready.

Stomping up the stairs, still toting her rumpled train, she paused at the upper landing, puzzled. The door to the spare room was closed. Sounds inside told her Clay was undressing there instead of using her personal bedroom, as she'd supposed he would.

Fine. There was no hurry. She'd change out of the cumbersome gown into the plain beige sheath she'd chosen for the reception and then wait for him to challenge her.

Slamming the door to her room, Sami shed her veil, tossed it onto the bed, then reached around to draw down the zipper of the snug-fitting satin dress. She held her breath. If the zipper got stuck, she'd have to phone Eleanor for help, because no way was she going to ask Clay.

Luckily, all went well and Sami slid her arms out of the long, lacy sleeves, letting the body of the gown drop on top of the billowing skirt at her feet. As soon as she and Clay had reached an understanding and were finished arguing, she'd go down and wait for the caterers.

Sami slipped the sheath over her head, added a gold belt and earrings, and changed her shoes. Running a brush through her hair, then refreshing her lipstick, she wondered what was taking Clay so long. Waiting like this was driving her crazy.

Impatient for the chance to assert herself, to let him know exactly where she stood, Sami left the sanctity of her bedroom and hurried down the hall to where she'd last heard him moving about.

Flinging open the bedroom door, her teeth clenched, her hands closing into tight fists, she stared, ready for anything.

Her jaw dropped. Good Lord! The room was empty.

Chapter Thirteen

Stomping down the stairs, still unable to believe he'd left her alone on purpose, Sami found Clay out on the front porch, rehanging the glider by himself and having a hard time getting it level.

"Need some help?" she asked, coming up behind him in time to hear some of his colorful epithets.

He looked her up and down appreciatively, then turned away. "No. You'll get all dirty."

"Okay. Suit yourself." She leaned against the newly refurbished porch railing, her arms crossed, and watched him work. He'd changed into slacks and a sport shirt, but he looked every bit as enticing as he had in the tux. It was clear to Sami that Clay's clothes were not the problem—her vivid imagination was.

Finishing, he checked both ends of the swing for height and stood back to admire his handiwork. "I revarnished it," he said. "The wood was badly weathered."

"I know. This place was in need of a lot of things till you showed up." Pausing, she decided to give him the full credit he deserved. "Without your help, I know these walls would have eventually collapsed around me."

"An old house needs serious upkeep."

Sami sighed. "Yes. That's why I think we should sell this place and move into yours."

"But you love it here."

"I know." She was nodding thoughtfully. "I'm also more practical than you are. We don't need two houses. One good one is plenty."

"The public schools may be better in Redlands," Clay said. "Maybe we should look into that first, then decide."

"School." Staring off into space, she considered his suggestion. "I suppose you're right. It seems like only yesterday that Jess was a tiny baby, so I suppose he'll be ready for kindergarten before I realize it."

"I wish I'd known him from the start," Clay confessed. "Sometimes I try to imagine what he was like but . . ."

Softening, Sami stepped closer and laid a hand on his arm. His skin was warm, inviting. The muscles twitched beneath her touch. "I really am sorry, Clay. I never meant to hurt you."

The timely arrival of the catered dinner gave him a perfect excuse to avoid commenting on her apology. The urge to take her in his arms and carry her up the stairs where they could be alone and truly begin their marriage was growing strong. He knew he'd either have to find better ways to distract himself or eventually leave the premises entirely.

Clay started for the driveway to direct the catering van to the rear for unloading. It was ironic he'd once accused Sami of trying to be a superwoman and now found himself struggling to become the male counterpart. They really were a pair, weren't they?

He glanced back. She was still standing right where he'd left her, her hands tightly clasped in front of her in her usual reaction to anxiety or tension. Oh God, she was beautiful! Clay thought. His whole body agreed in an instant, sending him into paroxysms of need so great he wondered how long he could continue to look at her and still preserve his sanity, let alone an outward calm.

Striding down the drive ahead of the slowly moving van, he physically took himself out of close proximity to Sami. It was a temporary respite but at this point he couldn't be choosy. Breathing heavily, he motioned to the driver. "Park it over there, by the garage."

The catering crew had set up tables ahead of time, then left to change into neat uniforms and pick up the food. Clay hung around long enough to get in their way and finally decided he'd run out of reasons to avoid returning to the house.

He was making his way slowly toward the back door when Jess barreled around the corner, spotted him and made a mad dash straight for him. Leaning down, Clay caught him, lifting him high overhead. "Hi, buddy."

Suddenly the little boy looked shyly away.

"Hey, what's the matter? You okay?" Clay asked, concerned.

Jess nodded while averting his face.

Balancing him on his hip, Clay carried him to a table beneath the arbor where a dish of pastel-colored mints and another of nuts had just been placed. He popped a yellow mint into his mouth. "I think the yellow ones are the best," he said as casually as he would have if Jess weren't upset. "Of course, the pink ones are the magic ones."

Jess peeked at the dish. "They are?"

"Yeah. They tell secrets."

The toddler cast him an unbelieving glance, then turned his concentration back to the dish of candy. "Really?"

"Sure," Clay said. "Here, I'll show you." Popping a pink mint into his mouth, he chewed it thoughtfully. "This one says it knows I'm glad to have you for my little boy."

"It does not."

"Oh, yes it does," Clay insisted. He gently rubbed the child's back to soothe him. "Let's try another one, shall we?"

"Okay."

"Umm. This one is even better."

Jess's eyes had begun to sparkle. "What does it say?"

"It says I love you and your mommy very much."

"No, you don't," Jess countered bravely. "Tommy and Travis said you can't love me because you're not my real daddy."

"I think that calls for another mint," Clay said, making the crucial decision based on what he felt was best for the boy. He chewed slowly, settling the matter in his mind before speaking. "This mint tells me I *am* your real daddy, but I'd love you even if that wasn't true."

"You are?" His small arms tightened around Clay's neck.

"Yes, Jess, I am." Tears of overwhelming happiness and gratitude to a benevolent Providence clouded his vision.

"Oh, wow!"

Clay kissed his soft, chubby cheek. Grinning broadly, he added, "Wow is right."

"You love me?"

"Of course I do."

"Mommy, too?"

Clay blinked to clear his eyes as best he could under the circumstances. "Yes, Jess, I love your mommy very, very much."

"Okay!" Squirming to get down, the little boy smiled at Clay as he pushed against his broad chest.

How wonderful it was to be a child, Clay thought, lowering him to the ground. When truth was presented in love, it was simply accepted, without question.

Watching his son run off so happily, he took a handkerchief from his pocket, wiped the dampness from his eyes and wished mightily that Sami was half as easy to deal with as the innocent, loving little boy.

Shivering in the thin sheath, Sami went inside to slip on an ivory sweater with a shawl collar as soon as the sun went down. Belting it, she returned to her guests.

Everyone seemed to be having a good time. Music was coming from a portable stereo, champagne was flowing freely, and the soft lighting in the garden provided a natural ambience.

Sami looked out over the crowd. Clay was standing by the punch bowl talking to a good-looking woman. In spite of her anxiety over the coming night, Sami felt she had to join him to find out who his companion was. They certainly did seem to be enjoying each other's company.

She stepped up beside Clay and smiled pleasantly before extending her hand to the other woman. "I'm Samantha. And you're...?"

"Judith Morrison. Clay's secretary. I believe we've spoken on the telephone." She shook Sami's hand. "I'm pleased to finally meet you."

Clay stood back and watched the exchange. It was polite enough. Still, there seemed to be an undercurrent he couldn't quite identify. When Sami put her hand through the crook of his elbow and took his arm possessively, he was certain something was wrong. One glance at the self-satisfied smirk on Judith's face told him she agreed and was pleased, rather than worried.

Could Sami be jealous? Clay wondered. His heart soared. Jealousy meant she cared, probably a lot more than she'd ever admitted to him. And she had once confessed to being in love with Jess's father. If that wasn't a part of her deception regarding the boy, maybe she really *did* love him. He certainly hoped so.

Raising her glass of champagne in an informal toast, Judith excused herself and joined Dick Rasmussen.

Clay felt Sami's grip on his arm loosen and placed his hand over hers to prolong the contact. "Don't go," he said. "I like having you close to me."

"Being married feels funny," she said quietly. "This is the same house, the same yard, even some of the same people we see every day, and yet we're not the same."

"No, we're not."

"I'm afraid," Sami admitted.

Clay stroked her hand beneath his, racking his brain for some word, some phrase, that would reach all the way into her guarded psyche and free her to truly become his wife. "I'll never hurt you, Sami. I know I swore that before, but it goes double now. You have to try to trust me."

"I do," she said. "It's me I have doubts about."

"Well, don't. We both came into this marriage with a lot of excess baggage. If we have to get rid of it one suitcase at a time, then that's how we'll do it."

"I think I have more of a steamer trunk," she quipped. "Or maybe a moving van."

"I don't care if you've brought along a whole damn freight train, honey. You're mine and that's all that counts." He gazed fondly into her eyes. "Have you forgiven me for not taking your last-minute confession seriously enough?"

She shrugged. "I don't know. I guess so. It's really a moot point now, anyway, isn't it?"

"It always was," Clay told her, his voice gentle. "Nothing anybody said or did could have kept me from going through with our wedding." He paused to give her time to digest that statement before continuing. "A little while ago, I told Jess I was his real father."

Sami was incredulous. "You *what?*"

"The Truesdale kids had been teasing him, and I felt it was best he learned the truth from me."

"How dare you do that without asking me first."

"I would have, but Jess was already real upset. I chose to put his mind at ease before the whole thing got blown way out of proportion."

"What could anybody possibly have said that warranted your speaking up like that?" Sami withdrew her hand from his arm and stepped back to confront him head-on.

"Jess was convinced I couldn't love him unless I was his real father."

"And you told him you were? Just like that?"

"No. I remembered a silly little trick my father used to pull on me years ago and I pretended to be able to discover the truth by magic." He explained the pink mints and Jess's reactions. "It was a harmless ruse, and it helped the poor kid open up and tell me what was bothering him."

"So that's what made you decide to confess?"

"Yes. And I'd do the same again if Jess needed convincing that he's loved."

"What about me?" Sami asked, blinking back tears. "If he thinks you can't love him unless you're his real father, then what's he going to do when he finds out I'm not his birth mother?"

"He'll be fine. I know he deserves to hear the entire story in the long run, just don't hit him with too much reality all at once, okay? When the time is right, you and I will sit him down and explain. He's known your love all his life. He won't doubt it now."

"Is that all you told him?" Sami asked, trembling.

Clay took her by the shoulders and looked deeply into her misty eyes. "No. I also told him I loved you, very, very much."

"Sometimes love isn't enough," she whispered, the background noise and music almost drowning out her words.

"I'll make it enough," Clay vowed. "I swear it." Bending down, he placed a conciliatory kiss on her forehead. "I love you more than life, Samantha."

"Oh, Clay. What am I going to do with you?"

"Love me back," he said softly.

For the second time that day, his heart leapt when he heard her say, "I do."

Jess had dozed off while playing hide-and-seek with the other children. He'd crawled under the buffet table, and the long tablecloth had hidden him so well, the Truesdale kids had given up and gone home without ever locating him.

When Sami realized he was missing, she was so distraught she was nearly frantic. Jess had never wandered off like that before. Concern for his safety was why she'd had the backyard fenced in the first place. Could he have gone with one of their guests? Had he slipped away unseen when the other children left?

"Calm down. We'll find him," Clay said, but Sami could tell he was as worried as she was.

She took his hand for moral support and felt him squeeze her fingers hard. "He's so little and helpless. Oh, Clay, what if something's happened to him?"

"Wherever he is, he's fine. Think. Where did we see him last?"

"Playing with Travis, I guess." She chewed on her lower lip. "I don't know."

"And you talked to Eleanor? Her kids have no idea where Jess might be?"

"None. I phoned her house as soon as we knew he was missing. She said they were all playing and Jess just disappeared."

The caterers had loaded the van with most of their supplies and were folding the large linen cloths when she and Clay spotted the sleepy toddler. Falling to their knees on the grass, they gathered his warm, drowsy body between them and held him close, rocking back and forth and hugging each other in the process.

Sami wasn't at all surprised to find she was crying. It did shock her, however, to see a trace of tears in Clay's eyes, too. Dear Lord, he did love Jess.

And she loved them *both* more than she'd ever imagined possible, she finally admitted. When she and Clay thought they'd lost Jess, the meaning of *family* became crystal clear. It was never supposed to be one parent pitted against the other for the child's affection, it was everybody together, loving everybody else as much as they possibly could.

Sami held tightly to her son and husband, rejoicing in their newly realized rapport. She felt Clay's arm circling her, pulling her closer, and she had no desire whatsoever to flee. Laying her head on his shoulder, she wept for joy.

He placed a kiss on her hair, then closed his eyes and tilted his head back, letting himself imagine what it would be like to hold her to him all night long and share their love the way a man and wife were meant to. Inside his soul, he knew Sami did care for him, now more than ever. All he had to do was create a nonthreatening opportunity for her to show him. Somehow.

Not wanting to let go of Jess after the fright he'd given them, both Sami and Clay took him up to bed. The little boy was still a bit groggy but not totally unaware of his surroundings.

Once he was settled in his pajamas, the lightweight covers laid loosely over him, he threaded his arms around Sami's neck and gave her a juicy kiss. "Night, Mama."

"Good night, sweetheart."

Looking past her as she stood to leave, Jess spotted Clay and held out his small arms to him, too.

Clay responded. Leaning down, he gave the tired little boy a good-night kiss and smoothed his hair off his forehead. "Night, buddy."

Jess smiled. "Call me sweetheart, like Mama does."

Chuckling, Clay shook his head. "If you want to call me Daddy, though, you sure can."

He seemed to think about the offer. "Okay. Night, Daddy." Hunkering down in his bed, he pulled the covers up under his chin and closed his eyes peacefully with a smile on his face.

Deeply touched, Clay followed Sami out of the room into the hall. They paused, silently studying each other. "Well, I guess this is it," he said, stuffing his hands in his pockets.

"Yes, I guess it is."

"Did you have a good time today?"

Sami smiled slightly and nodded. "To tell you the truth, it's all kind of a fuzzy blur."

"Yeah. I know what you mean. I'm sorry we can't take a honeymoon right away. Judith really chewed me out over it, but I can't leave the Sycamore project till more things are settled. You do understand, don't you?"

"Of course." Sami didn't intend to tell him how thrilled she'd been to learn they wouldn't immediately be sailing off somewhere to be alone. The coming nights were going to be hard enough to cope with in familiar surroundings. A strange room in a strange city was bound to make her adjustment to married life harder—and there was the fact she might not have anywhere to run to in an emergency.

Which could also be a problem tonight, she thought nervously. Her conscience had bothered her so much when she'd started to leave some of her personal things in the spare room, she'd abandoned the idea. Now that she was faced with Clay in person, every masculine inch of him, she was sorry she'd backed down.

"Well . . ." she drawled.

"Yeah, well."

"I guess I'd better be getting ready for bed." The normally innocuous statement almost stuck in Sami's dry throat. Why couldn't she have just bid him a simple goodnight the way she'd been rehearsing all day?

Clay saved her from any further explanation or embarrassment. "I'll go down and settle with the caterers, make sure they've got all their stuff loaded, then lock up the house for you."

"Good idea." *Good idea? How profound.* Her sudden lack of useful conversational skills left Sami wondering if she'd ever be able to feel totally at ease with Clay. And mentioning bed? Good God, why didn't she just invite the man to sleep with her and be done with it?

Because she wouldn't have to ask him, she answered effortlessly. He was her husband. He'd expect her to act like a wife. Even though he knew her past, Sami was certain he'd want them to be joined.

The idea of a physical union made her shiver. Before she could decide how to explain to Clay that she wasn't yet ready to make love, he surprised her by turning and walking away.

Sami wrapped her arms around herself and stood very still. In the quiet of the house she heard him descend the stairs, traverse the hall and exit through the back door.

But he'd be back, she knew, and when he returned, she hoped she didn't have to hurt his feelings to make him understand. Their recent closeness and touching had proved that kind of affection no longer bothered her the way it once had. In fact, she found Clay's nearness so pleasurable it made her innermost being ache in a way that was new to her.

Taking a deep, shaky breath, Sami forced herself to think about other things. Eleanor had given her a sheer white peignoir which she had no intention of wearing, not that her nightgown would make much difference. Short of locking herself inside a suit of armor, there was no way she was going to keep Clay out of her bed and away from her body. She knew that as surely as she'd known she was destined to be Jess's mother.

Closing her eyes, she stood quietly for a moment to gather strength, then started slowly for her room and the fate which awaited her there.

Chapter Fourteen

Clay paced the yard, wishing he had something constructive to do to occupy his time and take his mind off Sami. She was probably safely in bed by now, he thought, feeling his body grow taut, ready, but he'd give her another half hour just to be sure.

He checked his watch. Their wedding day had officially ended minutes before. Lord, he hoped giving her the ultimatum had been the right thing to do. Sometimes Sami seemed almost ready to accept the love he had to offer, yet at other times he sensed unreasonable fear lingering just beneath the surface of her otherwise calm appearance.

They had both sidestepped any mention of postmarital sleeping arrangements or of his moving in with her for the present. Clay knew avoiding such a frank discussion was probably a mistake, but he hadn't wanted to press the issue and have Sami back out of the marriage because of it.

Whatever she wanted to do, however fast or slow she needed him to be, he'd try to comply, even if it killed him.

She'd been through enough hell already. He loved her. He wasn't going to force her to do anything before she was ready.

Getting an overnight bag out of his car, he took it into the house, locking the door behind him. The old place had always had a welcoming air about it, he thought, even back when he was a kid.

Pausing at the foot of the staircase, Clay took a deep breath. Lingering aromas of food, lemon furniture polish and the everyday fragrances of living greeted him. This was what home should smell like, he mused, starting to climb the stairs. And feel like. In spite of the sacrifice he was going to make tonight, and for as many nights to come as necessary, this place and these loved ones were still the first real home he'd had since childhood. This was where he belonged.

At the top of the stairs, he paused. Light shone out from under Sami's door. Her signal would have been clearer had she also doused the lamp, but the fact that the door was tightly closed told him enough. All right. He'd wait. Somehow.

Teeth clenched, hands balled into fists, his gut churning, Clay turned the opposite way and headed for the spare room. It was going to be one hell of a long night.

Sami had heard him come into the house. Perched on the edge of her four-poster bed, she'd listened to his footfalls coming closer and closer. Her breath caught, her heart pounding so loudly in her ears she could hardly discern his steps any longer.

Soon, she thought, her fingers clasped tightly in her lap. Soon Clay would come through that door and take her in his arms and she'd have to try to deal with whatever demands he made.

The word *sex,* popped into her head, then was quickly replaced with *lovemaking.* That was the critical difference, of course. Rationally, she knew that. It was just that she hadn't had the practical experience of separating the two before and wasn't at all sure she could do it now, even for Clay.

The house was strangely silent. Perhaps he was waiting out there for her to open the door. Standing on shaky legs, she smoothed the thick terry-cloth robe—she'd put it on after deciding to don Eleanor's gift, after all—and lifted her chin courageously. She *did* love Clay. More than words could describe. She'd be all right. For him, she could do this—she *would* do this.

Her hand closing on the brass knob, Sami turned it and drew open the door. Blinking to adjust to the blackness in the unlit hall, she whispered, "Clay?"

No answer came. Surely he'd be there, she reasoned. Where else would he go? Maybe to check on Jess? Padding softly down the corridor on bare feet, she peeked in on her sleeping son. All was peaceful. The night-light she always left burning clearly showed that the child was alone.

Sami pivoted, envisioning Clay's trip up the stairs. She was sure, without a doubt, that she'd heard him approaching. Hands on her hips, she stared toward the spare room where he'd gone to change after the ceremony. A thin beam of light was shining out under the door.

Her heartbeats were pounding in her temples, her breathing labored. What did he think he was doing? He'd told her he loved her, yet was choosing to sleep alone on his wedding night? Had he been lying all along when he said he wasn't marrying her simply to get to Jess? That idea galled her to the bone. What inexcusable effrontery!

Marching down to the spare room, she jerked open the door without knocking. Clay lay in bed, his upper torso naked, his lower half covered by a thin blanket. He'd been staring at the ceiling with his hands laced behind his head. Now he was sitting bolt upright.

He scowled at her. "What's the matter?"

"I don't know," Sami said. "You tell me."

"What are you talking about?"

"Me? Us?" She waved her hands in the air. "Hell, I don't know anymore." Calming herself as best she could, she folded her arms across her chest and stared at him. "I thought we were married."

"We are." A look of caution came over Clay's face. "Just exactly what is it you're trying to say?"

"Do you really love me?"

"Of course I do." His unfulfilled sexual desires were making him sound too gruff, he knew, but seeing Sami standing there, so close, so desirable, was driving him over the edge.

She stepped a bit closer, cutting the distance between them in half. "Then why didn't you come to my room tonight?"

"You had your door closed."

"So?"

Clay shrugged. The blanket still shrouded his lower torso but his manhood showed, anyway, and there was little he could do about it since his clothes were all piled out of reach on a chair by the bureau.

When he shifted his weight in the narrow bed, the springs creaked. "I didn't want you to feel trapped, Sami. That's all. I'm not superhuman. I can't be around you all the time and not want you."

"You do?"

Clay cursed under his breath. "Yes. I want you so much sometimes I have to leave the room to keep my hands off you. When you hugged me and Jess tonight, right after we found him, I thought I was going to burst. I need you, honey. I can't help myself."

Taking one step, then another and another, she stopped beside him. Her decision wasn't a conscious one, it simply seemed the most natural thing to do. "You're my husband now, Clay. You shouldn't feel you have to run from me."

Untying the sash to her robe, Sami slipped it off her shoulders and let it drop to the floor so that all she had on was the diaphanous outfit Eleanor had given her. It was far from opaque. The way it clung to her uplifted breasts and flowed loosely over her hips, she knew it left little to his imagination.

"Don't do this, Sami," he warned, "unless you're ready to go all the way. I don't know that I can stop myself once we get started."

She watched his chest heaving as he breathed, saw the sheen of perspiration on his forehead. "All I ask is that we try to take it slow to begin with," she said. "Give me time to get used to being a part of you." Turning slightly, she sat down on the edge of the bed.

Clay's hand rested on hers, then traveled up her arm and over her shoulders. Cupping the back of her neck, he urged her to lean down for a kiss.

The instant Sami felt the touch of his lips, she was transported back to the first ethereal kiss they'd shared. That was the moment when she'd begun to have hope she could someday overcome the damage that had been done to her. Breaking contact, she smiled so Clay would know she was all right and began to rain tiny, biting kisses all over his neck while he stroked her back.

Caressing the bare skin of his chest, she toyed with the smattering of curly dark hair and traced her fingernail around his nipple before kissing him there, too.

Clay's resulting moan entered her ears, but came to rest somewhere far deeper inside. No longer timid, Sami pushed him down and lay across his chest, her hair tickling his cheek, her breasts pressed to him through the thin garment.

"I want us to try," she said quietly, sensuously.

His voice was husky, breathless. "Are you sure?"

"Yes." Sami laid her cheek on his chest, listening to his pounding heart and thinking about how much she loved him while attempting to block out the remnants of the old evil still clouding her soul. She reached to turn off the bedside lamp.

Clay stopped her by grasping her wrist. "Leave it on—at least the first time."

"Why?"

"Because I want you to be able to look at me, to know this is *me* and this is *love*, not anything else. Never anything else." He urged her hand back to his chest. "Please, Sami?"

She nodded.

"Then stand up."

As soon as she complied, he swept back the blanket and held out his hand to her, and she came to lie beside him in the crook of his arm, nestled against his ribs. She'd seen his whole body in those long seconds when he'd lifted the covers for her, and it was magnificent, not forbidding as she'd assumed. But then, this was Clay, not anyone else, and that obviously made all the difference.

"What do you want me to do?" Sami asked.

He placed a tender kiss on the top of her head and held her close. "Nothing. Everything. Do whatever feels good to you."

She laughed softly in sheer relief. "So far, everything has felt marvelous."

"I want you to tell me if I do or say anything that bothers you."

Sami pressed her palm to his warm chest and snuggled closer. "I will. I'm pretty naive about this kind of thing, though." She blushed and hid her face. "The love part, I mean."

"Good. Ever since we were kids I've dreamed of making beautiful love with you. In a way, this is my first time, too."

He kissed her then, rolling her atop his body and wrapping both strong arms around her to do it. Sami was instantly aware of the hard pressure of his evident desire against the softness of her abdomen. This is Clay, she reminded herself. This is Clay and he loves you. You don't have to be afraid anymore.

His body felt even bigger and more exciting than it had looked a few moments before. Taking a deep breath and putting all her trust in him, she moved slightly against his pelvis the way nature urged and was astounded to find how much she loved the feeling of power his instinctively primal reflexes gave her.

Tracing his hands over her ribs and up under her arms, he was soon cupping both breasts in his palms, his thumbs doing extraordinary things to her sensitive nipples through the bodice of the gown.

Sami clutched at him, her nails digging into his skin, her hungry mouth devouring his more eagerly than he'd ever dared hope.

"Oh, Clay!" she gasped. "Oh, Clay... love me."

She'd placed one leg between his, pushing herself against him till he thought he might actually lose control. Reaching down, he raised the hem of her gown till it no longer separated them and gently touched her. She was so warm and ready, he had to clench his teeth to keep from taking her right then, as they lay.

Exploring, teasing, moving as slowly as his colossal hunger would permit, he inched his fingers closer and closer to the seat of her desire. Sami flinched once, he retreated, and she reached down to press his hand closer.

"It's all right," she whispered, her voice husky with passion. "Touch me, Clay. Touch me again."

Slipping his fingers into the soft curls, he cupped her mound and held her, easing closer and closer till he'd reached his tender goal. "Does that hurt?"

Sami shook her head. Following his lead, she held her breath and lifted her hips just enough to slide her hand between their bodies. Her fingers sought him out and closed around him, breaking the last taboo she'd feared she wouldn't be able to face.

He was hard and silky at the same time, she discovered, his shaft pulsing with need, the softness below drawn up tight beneath the dark whorls of hair. Touching, caressing, exploring, she felt the life force within him straining to get out.

"Now," she whispered.

Clay rolled her over and positioned himself over her. The gown had slipped down again. Sami helped him lift it.

"You're sure?" he asked, praying she wouldn't change her mind.

Reaching up to cradle his slightly beard-roughened cheeks in her hands, she smiled and lifted her hips to meet his as she answered him with a deep, possessive kiss.

Clay instinctively probed for an instant, then gritted his teeth and forced himself to go slowly. Sami was probably as ready as she'd ever be, he noted, but there was still the final emotional barrier to overcome. If he frightened her now, it might be a long time before she'd be willing to try again.

Her warmth caressed him, the musky odor sending his senses reeling. Slowly, inch by inch, he entered her, watching her face for signs of distress while reveling in the sensation of drowning in her sweetness, of making them truly one.

"Still okay?" he asked quietly.

A sheen of perspiration covered his forehead. She wiped it away with her fingertips and nodded. "Am I making this too hard on you?"

He shook his head. "No. Nothing is too hard when we love each other." Almost seated completely within her, Clay was surprised when Sami reached down, cupped his buttocks in her hands and pulled him to her the rest of the way. With a groan, he fought to postpone the inevitable and nearly failed.

"Don't do that again, honey, or I won't be able to stop."

Totally enraptured with the intensity of their shared passion and the eroticism of the moment, she did exactly what he'd cautioned her not to do and lifted her hips once again, her nails digging into his back, her femininity closing tightly around him.

Clay was lost. He answered her primitive plea with a hard thrust, then another and another, rocking against her and burying himself to the hilt.

This wasn't happening the way he'd planned it, he thought, unable to convince his body that his rational mind should remain in control. His loins kept insisting that if Sami was okay, then there was no reason to hesitate.

He studied her through the haze of passion enshrouding him. Her lips were parted, her breath on his face so sweet it made him dizzy with desire. She was looking directly at him, the love and trust in her eyes complete and without reservation.

Clay knew there must have been a question in his expression, because she gasped, "Yes!" and sent him spiraling over the edge of the last vestiges of his self-control.

Words were woefully inadequate to describe something as marvelous as that moment, Sami thought as her back arched, every muscle in her body in tune with the instinctive contractions of his. After this night together, she and Clay would never be the same, nor would they want to be. It was as if they had each placed an invisible brand on the other, a brand of infinite, undying love.

He crested and she felt herself following. The breath she'd been unconsciously holding escaped in a cry of ecstasy which Clay quickly covered with his mouth, drinking in her final gasp and mingling it with a soul-deep utterance of his own.

Pleasured beyond belief, Sami stared up at him, her eyes wide, her lips love-bruised, her lungs still trying to make up for the total exertion of her body. An indescribable euphoria engulfed her. It was over. She'd beaten the demons. She was free!

Tears of happiness filled her eyes, then spilled over to run silently over her temples and into her hair. Wrapping her arms tightly around Clay's neck, she pulled him down onto her and clung to him, sobbing with relief.

Concerned, Clay rolled over, taking her with him and lifting her to lie atop his body where his greater weight wouldn't cause her further distress. "Oh, honey, I'm sorry. I was afraid that would happen. There's no good excuse. I've just wanted you for so long I couldn't control myself." He buried his face in her damp, tousled hair and pressed his lips to her neck.

Sami raised herself on her arms and began to laugh through her tears. "Sorry? I hope not. I sure hope not, because I'm going to expect a repeat performance any minute now."

He scowled up at her. "What?"

"Sex," she said, no longer afraid to speak the word when it was for his ears. "Good, old-fashioned, break-the-slats-in-the-bed loving."

"You aren't mad or hurt?" He brushed at her tears with his thumbs, hoping with all his heart that he understood what he thought she was trying to tell him.

"No!" Sami sniffled and rained kisses all over his face and neck. "No, no, no." When she raised up to gaze at him through the eyes of love, her grin was wider and more euphoric than he'd ever seen it before.

She rolled off him and lay prostrate in the narrow bed, her arms outstretched, her eyes closed. "I feel so wonderful!"

"In that case . . ." Clay got to his feet, reached down and scooped her up in his arms, swinging her legs across his chest and starting for the door, his happy burden clinging to him.

Traversing the hall, Clay nudged open the door to her room with his knee, then stepped through, his new wife still nestled against him. He pushed the door shut behind them with one foot.

Lowering Sami onto the four-poster bed, Clay drew his finger across her cheek to tuck a lock of silky hair behind her ear. "I love you, Samantha. More than ever."

"I love you, too," she said. "Tell me again that you don't mind not having more children. I need to hear it."

Clay raised on one elbow and gazed tenderly down at her. "I was going to save this for later, but since you brought it up, I'll tell you what I've been looking into. I've already talked to my lawyers about private adoption. I know there must be a beautiful little girl somewhere out there who'd make a great sister for Jess, if you agree that's what we should do."

Sami flung her arms around his neck. "Oh, it is! I just never dreamed you'd consider adopting."

"Why not?"

"I don't know. I guess because Jess is really yours."

"Is he?" Clay smiled down at her.

"Of course he is. He has to be. Vicki said . . ." Sami's eyes widened. "You think he's not? I suppose we could have him tested."

Clay was shaking his head, his heart overflowing with love and gratitude. "Don't you see, honey? It doesn't matter with Jess and it won't matter if we adopt other kids. We're a *family*. Lots of folks with blood ties live together in the same house and never manage to accomplish that. I know what's really important and what's not.''

Tears of joy and total relief began to cloud Sami's vision. "So do I," Sami said as she bent to kiss him. "Believe me, so do I...."

*   *   *   *   *

COMING NEXT MONTH

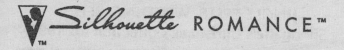 **Silhouette** ROMANCE™

BELIEVING IN MIRACLES
by
Linda Varner

Carpenter Andy Fulbright and Honorine "Honey" Truman had all the criteria for a perfect marriage—they liked and respected each other, they desired and needed each other...and *neither* one loved the other! But with the help of some mistletoe and two young elves, these two might learn to believe in the miracle of Christmas....

BELIEVING IN MIRACLES is the second book in Linda Varner's MR. RIGHT, INC., a heartwarming series about three hardworking bachelors in the building trade who find love at first sight—construction site, that is!

Don't miss BELIEVING IN MIRACLES, available in December. And look for Book 3, WIFE MOST UNLIKELY, in March 1995. Read along as old friends make the difficult transition to lovers....

Only from **Silhouette**®

where passion lives.

JINGLE BELLS, WEDDING BELLS:
Silhouette's Christmas Collection for 1994

Christmas Wish List

*To beat the crowds at the malls and get the perfect present for *everyone,* even that snoopy Mrs. Smith next door!

*To get through the holiday parties without running my panty hose.

*To bake cookies, decorate the house and serve the perfect Christmas dinner—just like the women in all those magazines.

*To sit down, curl up and read my Silhouette Christmas stories!

Join *New York Times* bestselling author Nora Roberts, along with popular writers Barbara Boswell, Myrna Temte and Elizabeth August, as we celebrate the joys of Christmas—and the magic of marriage—with

JINGLE BELLS, WEDDING BELLS

Silhouette's Christmas Collection for 1994.

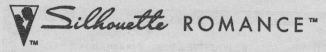
Silhouette ROMANCE™

'Tis the season for romantic bliss.
It all begins with just one kiss—

UNDER THE MISTLETOE

Celebrate the joy of the season and the thrill of romance with this special collection:

#1048 ANYTHING FOR DANNY by Carla Cassidy—Fabulous Fathers
#1049 TO WED AT CHRISTMAS by Helen R. Myers
#1050 MISS SCROOGE by Toni Collins
#1051 BELIEVING IN MIRACLES by Linda Varner—Mr. Right, Inc.
#1052 A COWBOY FOR CHRISTMAS by Stella Bagwell
#1053 SURPRISE PACKAGE by Lynn Bulock

Available in December, from Silhouette Romance.

SRXMAS

SILHOUETTE... Where Passion Lives

Don't miss these Silhouette favorites by some of our most distinguished authors! And now you can receive a discount by ordering two or more titles!

SD#05750	BLUE SKY GUY by Carole Buck	$2.89 ☐
SD#05820	KEEGAN'S HUNT by Dixie Browning	$2.99 ☐
SD#05833	PRIVATE REASONS by Justine Davis	$2.99 ☐
IM#07536	BEYOND ALL REASON by Judith Duncan	$3.50 ☐
IM#07544	MIDNIGHT MAN by Barbara Faith	$3.50 ☐
IM#07547	A WANTED MAN by Kathleen Creighton	$3.50 ☐
SSE#09761	THE OLDER MAN by Laurey Bright	$3.39 ☐
SSE#09809	MAN OF THE FAMILY by Andrea Edwards	$3.39 ☐
SSE#09867	WHEN STARS COLLIDE by Patricia Coughlin	$3.50 ☐
SR#08849	EVERY NIGHT AT EIGHT by Marion Smith Collins	$2.59 ☐
SR#08897	WAKE UP LITTLE SUSIE by Pepper Adams	$2.69 ☐
SR#08941	SOMETHING OLD by Toni Collins	$2.75 ☐

(limited quantities available on certain titles)

TOTAL AMOUNT	$_____
DEDUCT: 10% DISCOUNT FOR 2+ BOOKS	$_____
POSTAGE & HANDLING ($1.00 for one book, 50¢ for each additional)	$_____
APPLICABLE TAXES*	$_____
TOTAL PAYABLE (check or money order—please do not send cash)	$_____

To order, complete this form and send it, along with a check or money order for the total above, payable to Silhouette Books, to: **In the U.S.:** 3010 Walden Avenue, P.O. Box 9077, Buffalo, NY 14269-9077; **In Canada:** P.O. Box 636, Fort Erie, Ontario, L2A 5X3.

Name:_____

Address:_____ City:_____

State/Prov.:_____ Zip/Postal Code:_____

*New York residents remit applicable sales taxes.
Canadian residents remit applicable GST and provincial taxes.

SBACK-SN

Silhouette®

"HOORAY FOR HOLLYWOOD" SWEEPSTAKES

HERE'S HOW THE SWEEPSTAKES WORKS

OFFICIAL RULES — NO PURCHASE NECESSARY

To enter, complete an Official Entry Form or hand print on a 3" x 5" card the words "HOORAY FOR HOLLYWOOD", your name and address and mail your entry in the pre-addressed envelope (if provided) or to: "Hooray for Hollywood" Sweepstakes, P.O. Box 9076, Buffalo, NY 14269-9076 or "Hooray for Hollywood" Sweepstakes, P.O. Box 637, Fort Erie, Ontario L2A 5X3. Entries must be sent via First Class Mail and be received no later than 12/31/94. No liability is assumed for lost, late or misdirected mail.

Winners will be selected in random drawings to be conducted no later than January 31, 1995 from all eligible entries received.

Grand Prize: A 7-day/6-night trip for 2 to Los Angeles, CA including round trip air transportation from commercial airport nearest winner's residence, accommodations at the Regent Beverly Wilshire Hotel, free rental car, and $1,000 spending money. (Approximate prize value which will vary dependent upon winner's residence: $5,400.00 U.S.); 500 Second Prizes: A pair of "Hollywood Star" sunglasses (prize value: $9.95 U.S. each). Winner selection is under the supervision of D.L. Blair, Inc., an independent judging organization, whose decisions are final. Grand Prize travelers must sign and return a release of liability prior to traveling. Trip must be taken by 2/1/96 and is subject to airline schedules and accommodations availability.

Sweepstakes offer is open to residents of the U.S. (except Puerto Rico) and Canada who are 18 years of age or older, except employees and immediate family members of Harlequin Enterprises, Ltd., its affiliates, subsidiaries, and all agencies, entities or persons connected with the use, marketing or conduct of this sweepstakes. All federal, state, provincial, municipal and local laws apply. Offer void wherever prohibited by law. Taxes and/or duties are the sole responsibility of the winners. Any litigation within the province of Quebec respecting the conduct and awarding of prizes may be submitted to the Regie des loteries et courses du Quebec. All prizes will be awarded; winners will be notified by mail. No substitution of prizes are permitted. Odds of winning are dependent upon the number of eligible entries received.

Potential grand prize winner must sign and return an Affidavit of Eligibility within 30 days of notification. In the event of non-compliance within this time period, prize may be awarded to an alternate winner. Prize notification returned as undeliverable may result in the awarding of prize to an alternate winner. By acceptance of their prize, winners consent to use of their names, photographs, or likenesses for purpose of advertising, trade and promotion on behalf of Harlequin Enterprises, Ltd., without further compensation unless prohibited by law. A Canadian winner must correctly answer an arithmetical skill-testing question in order to be awarded the prize.

For a list of winners (available after 2/28/95), send a separate stamped, self-addressed envelope to: Hooray for Hollywood Sweepstakes 3252 Winners, P.O. Box 4200, Blair, NE 68009.

CBSRLS

OFFICIAL ENTRY COUPON

"Hooray for Hollywood"
SWEEPSTAKES!

Yes, I'd love to win the Grand Prize — a vacation in Hollywood —
or one of 500 pairs of "sunglasses of the stars"! Please enter me
in the sweepstakes!

**This entry must be received by December 31, 1994.
Winners will be notified by January 31, 1995.**

Name _____

Address _____ Apt. _____

City _____

State/Prov. _____ Zip/Postal Code _____

Daytime phone number _____
                              (area code)

Account # _____

Return entries with invoice in envelope provided. Each book
in this shipment has two entry coupons — and the more
coupons you enter, the better your chances of winning!

DIRCBS

OFFICIAL ENTRY COUPON

"Hooray for Hollywood"
SWEEPSTAKES!

Yes, I'd love to win the Grand Prize — a vacation in Hollywood —
or one of 500 pairs of "sunglasses of the stars"! Please enter me
in the sweepstakes!

**This entry must be received by December 31, 1994.
Winners will be notified by January 31, 1995.**

Name _____

Address _____ Apt. _____

City _____

State/Prov. _____ Zip/Postal Code _____

Daytime phone number _____
                              (area code)

Account # _____

Return entries with invoice in envelope provided. Each book
in this shipment has two entry coupons — and the more
coupons you enter, the better your chances of winning!

DIRCBS